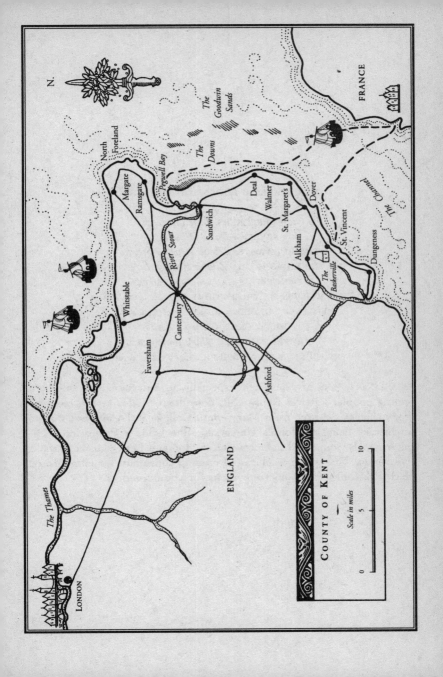

The SMUGGLERS

High Seas Trilogy, Book II

Iain Lawrence

A Dell Yearling Book

Published by
Dell Yearling
an imprint of
Random House Children's Books
a division of Random House, Inc.
1540 Broadway
New York, New York 10036

Visit us on the Web! www.randomhouse.com/kids

Educators and librarians, for a variety of teaching tools, visit us at
www.randomhouse.com/teachers

ISBN 0-440-41596-9

Reprinted by arrangement with Delacorte Press

Printed in the United States of America

October 2000

10 9 8 7

OPM

For my nephews and my nieces,
Andrew and Iain,
Lisa, Erin, and Shauna,
and all those who sailed with them
on the little ship Connection

CONTENTS

Chapter 1
THE HIGHWAYMAN

We raced across Kent in a coach-and-four, from London toward the sea. Over moonlit meadows and down forest roads as black as chimneys, we took a serpentine route through every little village. I and my father, and a man who never spoke.

"We're going miles from our way on this roundabout route," said Father, bouncing beside me. "I knew we should have stayed the night at Canterbury. I should have stuck to my guns."

"But I want to see this ship of yours," I said.

Father laughed. "Now, now. It isn't mine yet."

Father was a merchant, a landsman. He never thought of a ship as anything but "it." Once he had said, "What's a ship but a pile of wood and nails? Knock it together a different way, and you've built yourself a house."

"But what is she?" I now asked. "A brig? A barquentine?"

1

Father sighed. He held his cane across his lap, twisting it in his hands. "I believe it's a schooner. And it's painted black, if that helps."

In the moonlight his face was pale, and he seemed to shiver as the coach clattered onto a bridge just beyond Alkham. "It lies to an anchor," said he, "in the River Stour."

"Does she have topsails?" I asked.

"Topsails?" said Father. "Oh, I daresay it does. And an enormous great figurehead, too."

The coach rattled over the hump of the bridge like a box full of pegs. I heard a shout from the driver, and then the crack of his whip, and we swayed round a corner with the axles screeching. On the opposite seat our silent stranger slept, as he had all the way from Canterbury.

He was a gentleman, but a tiny one. Carefully combed, polished and shined, he looked like a doll that a child had dressed in gray clothes and propped there in the carriage. Though Father had to slouch to keep his head from touching the roof, the gentleman sat bolt upright in his tall beaver hat, his little feet side by side on a box of wood and leather. Mile after mile, he had not moved so much as a finger.

I continued my questioning. "What's she called? Does she have a name?"

"Of course it does, John," said Father. "I'm told it's called the *Dragon*."

The gentleman nearly jumped from his seat. "The *Dragon*?" he whispered. "Is it the *Dragon* you said?"

Father stared at him, astonished. "And what concern is that of yours?" he asked. "State your business, sir."

"You're in the trade, then?" said the gentleman. He glanced toward the window.

"Speak up!" said Father, leaning forward. "What trade?"

"The free trade." He covered his mouth and whispered through his fingers. "The smuggling."

"Confound you," said Father. "Who are you, sir?" If the carriage were bigger, he would have stood in it; he would have strutted through it, as he did through his office in London. "What's your name?" he demanded.

"Larson," said the gentleman. He looked to either side. "I'm . . . connected . . . with the trade."

"Then you should be hanged," said Father. He threw himself back against the seat, rapping his palm with his cane. "I'd do it myself; I gladly would."

Larson's hands went back to his lap. His feet, like small animals, made themselves comfortable on the top of his box. Then his eyes closed, and it was as though he had never moved at all. The carriage swept down a long hill, and the hooves of the horses thundered ahead. With a cry from the driver and a jangle of harness, we hurtled down into a forest of beech trees, and the moonlight vanished from the coach. But in the last flicker through the branches, I saw the gentleman smile.

"A word of advice," said he. "You stay clear of that ship. The *Dragon*."

I heard Father snort, a sound I knew well. I had seen his clerks cringe at that noise, whole rows of them turning their heads.

"She's bad luck," Larson continued. "No, she's worse than that. She's evil."

"How can a ship be evil?" I asked.

"I don't know," said he. "I'm only aware of the one that is."

The whip cracked and cracked again. The driver's shouts came quickly, shrill in the clatter of iron and wood. The horses, snorting, pulled us at a gallop, and black on black the trees went by. I could only imagine the speed, but it must have been at least ten miles an hour.

"A ship can't be evil," said Father. "That's nonsense."

"I hope so," said Larson, his voice nearly lost in the clamor. "At least I've warned you."

"And who are you to warn me?"

But Larson had no chance to answer. The horses screamed in sudden fright, and the carriage jolted heavily. I was thrown forward, nearly from my seat. Father's cane went spinning from his hands.

"What the devil?" said he.

A pistol shot exploded, cracking through the night. The carriage skittered sideways at such a speed that it tilted up on two wheels before falling flat again with a jarring bang of wood. As we came to a stop a second shot rang out, and in its echo cried a voice, taut with peril. "Stand and deliver!"

"Oh, Lord," said Father. "A highwayman."

In the darkness we could hear his boots tapping on the road. He came toward us step by step, and when he halted there was silence, a dreadful stillness I could feel. The moon shone through the trees with a light that was cold and flat, more awful than the darkness. It spilled in through the windows and made grim, white ghosts of Father and Lar-

4

son. And into that silent, eerie world fell a single sound, the cocking of a pistol.

Father touched my knee. "Whatever happens, John," he said, "you keep your tongue in your head. Understand?"

I nodded; I felt I couldn't speak if I wanted to. Father's fingers squeezed, then fell away. He said, "Perhaps it's the baggage he's after."

"I rather hope so," said Larson. He moved his feet from the box and bent forward to lift it to his lap. The highwayman came closer, the sound of his boots like the sound of the box's latches as Larson thumbed them open. "But I'm afraid it might be myself he wants."

"Driver, step down," said the highwayman. "Quickly now."

The coach rocked. There was a squeal of springs and the thud of heavy boots. A horse stomped and whinnied, and all the sounds of the forest returned, echoing through the trees.

Larson opened his box, and in the silvery glow of the moon I saw a pair of fancy dueling pistols nested there, a gleam of gold and polished wood. They were long-barreled, wicked in their beauty—the most sinister things I had ever seen.

Father stared at him. "Who *are* you?" he asked.

The little gentleman smiled. His hands shook very slightly as he took the pistols from his box. "I think I'm a dead man," he said. "Now or later, I'm a goner."

The harness jingled. A horse whinnied nervously. "Steady there, girl," said the driver softly, and the highwayman shouted, "Come out from the carriage!"

Father went first, with a last glance at me. Larson started

after him, and as he leaned past me he said in a voice so faint I could hardly hear, "The other side. The roof." He slipped a pistol into my hand. His voice was little more than a breath. "If it goes poorly for us, shoot him down like a dog." He slid to the door, and as he stooped to go through I saw the other pistol twinkle behind him, then vanish into the tails of his coat. He was a mysterious man, furtive as a spy, and I had no idea who he was or what he hoped to be. He went down the step with his hand on the brim of his beaver, down to the road beside Father.

I did as he said and went out through the opposite door. I climbed up to the roof of the carriage, and I crouched there among the boxes and the baggage. Below me, in a line, stood the driver, Father, and Larson. The highwayman stayed by the horses, lurking in their shadows.

He was a tall man in a flowing coat of a bright and fiery red. Bandoliers crossed his chest, and into them were stuffed half a score of pistols. He had others in his belt, and one in each hand. He bristled with pistols. His collars were turned up high, and he wore a flat and wide-brimmed hat that hid his face completely.

"A pretty poor turnout," he said. "A pretty poor one, indeed." He took a step forward—he swaggered, really—and stopped by the front of the coach. "Well, turn out your pockets," he said. "Show me the linings." Then, "Hop to it!" he shouted, and laughed. He shoved a pistol in the air and fired, and the flames shot up like a Roman candle. The horses, frightened, clanged against their harness.

"Watches, rings," said the highwayman. "Empty your purses and your pockets. I want to hear silver jingle. Silver and gold." He whirled on his heels and blasted another shot into the forest, then whirled back around as his hands, fast as a juggler's, replaced the pistols with new ones.

"Driver," he said. "What cargo?"

"Nothing," said the driver in a small and frightened voice. "The night coach don't carry no freight on account of—" He trembled, his cap in his hand. "Of the highwaymen, see."

"Well, that's ironical," said the highwayman. "Lord love me, that's rich." He laughed, and I thought then that the man was quite insane. He looked like a pirate in his big red coat, weighted down with enough pistols for a whole band of brigands. But he bowed and straightened, his sleeves billowing, and suddenly he seemed as harmless as a robin hopping on the road.

It was Larson who spoke. "There's nothing for you here," he said.

The highwayman took a step toward Larson. "And who made you foreman of the jury?" he asked.

Larson didn't move. His feet astride a little pile of jewels and coins, he faced the highwayman and said, "Let us pass, and we'll say no more about it."

The highwayman stepped slowly toward him, and even the horses turned their heads to watch. I lifted my hand. The pistol was light, yet it shook in my fist so badly that I had to brace my arm on the baggage rail.

Below me, the highwayman stopped a mere yard from Larson, towering above him. "Well, well," he said. "A little fancy gent. You'd think he just stepped down from a cuckoo clock."

Larson was in the middle, my father to his left, the driver to his right. He looked almost like a child between them. His hands went slowly, smoothly, around his back to his waist, toward the pistol at his belt.

"Look at him," said the highwayman to Father. "A proper dandy, isn't he? A bug in a hat."

"What do you want?" said Father. "You've got our money. You've got my watch." He nudged it with his cane. "Isn't that enough?"

"I think there's more," said the highwayman. "Driver, is there something else?"

"Something else?" asked the driver. He was terrified, I could see; he was shaking head to toe.

The highwayman stretched out his arm and set the muzzle of a pistol against the driver's heart. On the instant, the poor man seemed to crumble. He blurted out, "The boy! There's a boy in the carriage."

I stared down the long barrel of my pistol, and the beaded sight shivered across the highwayman's hat. With my thumb I drew back the flintlock. It snapped into place.

That tiny sound, the merest click, seemed to me as loud as cannons. The highwayman spun toward the carriage door. Larson reached for the pistol at his waist, and Father—not knowing it was there—threw himself toward the highwayman. I saw a blur of red; I pulled the trigger. And at the same instant the highwayman's pistol flared and smoked; I watched him shoot my father.

It all happened in the blink of an eye, yet it lasted forever. In the glare from my own pistol, I saw the highwayman's finger squeeze the trigger. I watched the hammer fall, the powder flash. I saw the flames come bright as sunlight from the barrel.

Father staggered back. His cane fell to the ground and his hands clutched at his heart. Then his legs buckled under him, and he dropped in a heap to the road.

It was all madness and confusion. The highwayman turned and ran; Larson fired after him. Then a huge black horse reared up from the forest and thundered past the carriage, the highwayman clinging to its back like an enormous crimson lizard. And it was only then that I really heard the noise of this one long moment. It rushed over me with the smell of powder—the shots, the shouts, the pounding of that great black beast's hooves. It roared inside my head, a din that nearly deafened me.

Chapter 2
A WARNING

I dropped the pistol and clambered down from the coach to Father. He was lying with his legs bent under him, breathing short and shallow gasps. A wisp of smoke rose from his jacket, between the fingers he held tight to his heart. He smelled of gunpowder as I dropped to my knees and then across him; I blubbered like a child.

The driver came and lifted me off. His hands at my shoulders, he pulled me away. Then he held me, and over and over he said, "I'm sorry, I'm so terribly sorry."

Father's watch, his coins, his favorite ring lay scattered across the road. Larson picked them up, every one, using his beaver hat as a collection bowl. Without a word, he set this down beside me, then turned to see to Father.

He was so tender and gentle. He took Father's fingers from their terrible clutch across his breast, then felt with those small hands along ribs and chest, through jacket and waistcoat. "Hmmm," he said, and then, "Oh, my," and last, "I don't know how it happened."

In the driver's arms, I shook my head. "Nor do I." It seemed unreal, as though in a moment I would find myself still inside the carriage, bouncing across Kent with my father beside me. I would wake from a dream of a man in red, a man on a midnight horse.

"The scoundrel shot at point-blank range," said Larson. "The powder has burned your father's coat to cinders. But underneath there's not a mark, not a scratch; there's nothing."

I could hardly understand what the man was saying. Even his voice seemed unnatural, so great was my shock. It sounded hollow and distant.

"He's had the fright of his life," said Larson. "Fainted dead away." His hands picked scorched threads from Father's coat. "But he'll be right as rain if we can get him somewhere warm. Let him rest before the trembles start."

"I know of an inn," said the driver. "It's not an hour from here." He stood so quickly that I fell from his arms and sprawled across the road. Then he put down a hand and smiled in a funny way. "You see, sonny," he said, "it all works out for the best. All for the best in the end."

Just how that was I couldn't quite fathom. But soon we were rattling down the same road, Larson and I facing backward, staring at Father as he lay on the opposite bench. In a weird and restless sleep, Father moaned and sighed; he twitched his arms as though to shield himself. On the floor,

11

his watch and coins jingled in the bowl of Larson's hat, and the moonlight came and went. The horses ran at a furious pace as we hurtled through the forest, through fields and orchards, south and east toward the sea.

"He'll be fine," said Larson. "Don't you worry, John." And then, perhaps to get my mind on something else, he asked about our journey. "What brings you down to Kent?"

I told him about Father's business as a merchant, and the ships he owned in London. I told him about the *Isle of Skye* and how we'd come to lose her—and nearly our lives as well—to the wreckers of Pendennis. "My father's not old," I said, "but he must use a cane now, because of what happened to him there. The rats; they chewed his foot."

Though he was twice my sixteen years, Larson listened to my story the way a boy would, all eagerness. And then he asked, "So now he's buying the *Dragon*?"

"He hopes to," said I.

The little gentleman shook his head. "I can't imagine such wealth."

"It's not like that," I told him. "Father lost a fortune with the *Isle of Skye,* and every penny he has will go toward the *Dragon.* If he loses her as well—" The thought scared me. "He'll be ruined, Mr. Larson. Absolutely ruined."

"I see," said Larson. He leaned forward, across the carriage, and fussed at Father's jacket. "Then for what it's worth," he said, "I'll tell you again to steer clear of that ship, young John. She'll bring you trouble and misery. She'll bring you death."

"My death?" I asked.

"Maybe yours," said he. "Maybe others'. But death she'll bring you, and I'll promise you that. It's the way of a ship that was christened with blood."

He would tell me no more. When I tried to continue the conversation, he pretended not to hear.

The carriage came upon a village, and we sped along through winding streets. The driver shouted and cracked his whip, and Father came awake. He jolted from his dreams with an awful scream, and his arms flew up before him.

"Easy now," said Larson. "Just lie and rest, Mr. Spencer. I think we're almost there."

Around a corner, around another; I could hear the horses panting. And at last the carriage crossed a bridge and came to a stop before an old brick inn. It was called the Baskerville, and it rose two stories from a stone foundation, as cheerless as a prison.

The driver came down with a lantern and opened the carriage door. He was gray with dust, shimmering in the light as he moved and the dust fell away from his arms and legs. With Larson on one side and I on the other, holding the cane, we helped Father out of the coach and toward a doorway set deep in the wall. The driver hurried ahead and pounded on the door with a big iron knocker. The sound boomed through the inn.

Father slumped between us. He had the trembles, and they shook right through my arms, right through Larson's, as though all three of us were shivering.

Again the driver hammered. "Hallo!" he shouted. "Hallo, the inn!"

We heard footsteps on the other side, then the scraping of the latches. And a woman's voice, old as the grave, hailed us through the wood. "Who's there?" she asked. "Fleming, is it you?" The hinges squealed. "Oh, Flem, at last it's you?"

She was short, brittle, crooked as a walking stick. Her hair, the silvery gray of ashes, was thin across her skull. Her eyes were pale and empty-looking; the woman was blind. She came lurching out through the door like a mole from its burrow, feeling ahead of her along the wood and the stone. She carried a traveler's bag of canvas and leather, and I stared at it with a feeling of indescribable pity. For it was rotting in her hand.

The straps were worn to threads; the sides were as thin as lace. Insects and mice had eaten great holes in the bottom, and bits of clothing hung out, all frilly and black, but heavy with cobwebs. Yet she carried this thing, in the claw of her hand, as though she meant to hoist it up in the carriage and be off on her way.

"Fleming?" she asked again, more sadly than before.

"No, no, Mrs. Pye," said the driver. He shouted at her, as though she were deaf and not blind. "It's not your Fleming." He took her arm and turned her around. "I've brought a man who needs a meal and a bed. A man and his son, Mrs. Pye."

She put her satchel beside the door, on a patch of old carpet that was lighter-colored than all the rest—a place where it must have sat for many years. "Bring the fellow in," she said. "The captain's in the parlor, and I'll bring the suppers there." She shuffled off along a hallway, through the darkness of a coal mine. She had no need for candles, no use for lamps.

The driver watched her go. "Poor blind Mrs. Pye," he said. "Every knock on the door, every footstep, is her husband come back from the wars. She meets them all with that bag in her hand."

"How long has her husband been gone?" asked I.

"Nigh on thirty years." He started back to the carriage to fetch our luggage down. "She was only a guest then at the Baskerville," he said, climbing up. "There's a window high at the back looking over the sea, and there she would sit watching for Fleming. Any day, she thought, he would come and take her home to Romney." He hoisted our two small bags from the rack and tossed them down. Father flinched as they thudded on the ground.

"She went blind, and still she sat by that window," said the driver. "She's stayed so long, she's become a fixture. She runs the inn now, more or less."

By the time our bags were down, Father was walking. He was still a bit wobbly but stood supported only by his cane. "Up on his own pegs" was how the driver put it, with a great smile of pleasure. But when it came time to go inside the inn, Larson would not enter. "It wouldn't be wise," he said, as mysterious as he'd ever been. "Not wise for me nor you."

Father nearly begged him to stay, and urged the driver, too. He offered them food and drink, and even lodging if they wanted. But Larson couldn't get away quickly enough.

The little gentleman even left his hat behind, as a holder for Father's coins. He hopped up into the carriage and told the driver to hurry.

"You may see me again at Pegwell Bay," said he. "Watch for me, John."

He was right; I would indeed see him there. But it would be a strange and sad reunion.

Chapter 3
THE OLD CAPTAIN

The parlor of the Baskerville was an enormous room of oak and brick, a place of darkness and of shadows. The ceiling and the beams were blackened by soot, and only three lamps burned in the cavernous space. There was room in the hearth for a fire big enough to burn a witch, but only a tiny glimmer of embers came from there. The room was empty except for one man.

He looked up as Father and I came together through the door—up from a glass of brandy that he held in both hands, as though at any moment it might go sliding off across the table. He had a boat cloak drawn across his shoulders, but I didn't need that to tell me he was an old shellback. Every line on his face, every crook in his body, spoke of the sea. His eyes were so squinted by salt winds and sun that they seemed like dark little beads sewn among folds of leather. He looked at us, then looked away to fill his glass again with brandy and water.

Father settled down in a chair beside the hearth, then drew it even closer, until he sat nearly in the ashes. I took a poker from the gridiron and stirred the coals into a reddish glow. And Father held his hands toward it.

There was a hole in his jacket, almost round, where the highwayman's gun had seared through the cloth. Through it I could see his shirt, scorched as well, turned to yellow by the powder burns.

Father, seeing me staring, touched the hole with his fingers. He looked down at it, his beard going flat across his chest. "I knew they wove some amazing cloths on Threadneedle Street," said he. "But they've outdone themselves here. It must be strong as armor."

He was teasing me. I knew no linen in the world could turn aside a pistol ball.

"I suppose the gun misfired," said Father. "That brigand had a dozen pistols armed and ready, and he chose the only one that wouldn't work." He started shaking again. "I'd like to see him hang for this."

"Och, no, ye wouldna that!" The sailor's voice bellowed across the room, a Scottish accent blurred by drink. "Have ye ever seen a hanging, then? It's no a pretty sight, let me tell ye that."

Father looked up, startled. "I beg your pardon," he said. "I don't believe I know you."

"Captain Crowe," said the man in a fearsome shout, as though against a gale. "Captain Turner Crowe. And I've been to a hanging once. Someone near," said he, and surprised me with a bark of laughter. "Someone near and dear."

Father snorted. "If he was a scoundrel, he deserved it. I would hang every highwayman. And every smuggler, too."

"Och, ye'd be a busy man," said Captain Crowe.

"But a happy one," said Father. "An honest merchant can hardly make a living for all the trade that's done in the moonlight and the fog. If the smuggling goes on the way it is, I'll be in the poorhouse next, and half of London with me."

Poor old Mrs. Pye came into the room then, making a long journey of the trip from the pantry to the hearth. She brought us soup, a jug of water, and a loaf of bread as round and fat as a kettle. "Captain Crowe," she said, "could you help me, dear?" But I got up instead and took the tray that wobbled in her hands.

"Och, bring it here, lad," said Captain Crowe. He sat upright and drew his glass toward him. He invited us to share his table. "If ye think it's good enow for men o' London," said he. And Father—what choice did he have?—left the fire to sit there with the sailor.

The boat cloak was white with salt, as crusty as the bread. But the captain hauled it up around his neck, until it wrapped him like a shroud. "What brings you down to Kent?" he asked.

"A ship," said Father. "It's called the *Dragon*."

Across the room there came a clatter. "Mercy sakes!" said Mrs. Pye. She'd bumped against a table.

"Och, aye, the *Dragon*," said Captain Crowe in a hurried voice. "Sure I know the *Dragon*, and a fine old ship she is." He took a drink, eyeing us over the rim of the glass. "And

19

what is it, then, ye'd be wanting with her? If," said he, "I might be so bold as ask."

"I hope to buy that ship," said Father. "And John here will help me take it up to London."

"What, by yourselves?" asked Captain Crowe.

Father laughed. "I daresay that John would try it single-handed." He broke the bread and sopped it in the soup, then shook his head as he chewed and swallowed. "I hope to find a cargo—local goods, you see—and some men to handle the ship."

"She lies at Pegwell Bay?" the captain said.

Father nodded.

"Then it's round the Foreland for ye, lad, and mind that ye watch for the Goodwin Sands."

I asked, "What's that?"

"Whit's that?" the captain shouted. "Why, laddie, it were the ruin of the fleet a hundred years ago. Look," said he, "this is the shore of Kent." He dipped a finger in his brandy and drew a curving line across the table, toward his jug of water. He marked St. Vincent with a chunk of bread, and with another put London in the corner, right against Father's soup. "The *Dragon*'s here," he said, dropping down another bit, "and this is the Goodwin Sands." In his fist he ground a lump of bread, and the crumbs fell down across the table. He ground and ground, and the crumbs piled up in a crescent to the south and east. "Now," he said, and brushed his hand across his cloak, "one day they'll look like this, and I see what ye're thinking. 'Och, where's the danger in that?' ye ask. Weel, look, Mr. Spencer. The Sands are forever drifting, forever on the move. And so the next day—" He blew across the table, and the crumbs scattered. "—they'll look like this, ye see. There's few that know the way o' the Sands, and fewer yet who dare to find their way across them."

Father leaned forward, peering at the crumbs.

"In the great storm," the captain said, "the fleet was anchored in the Downs. That's here, ye see, just inland o' the Goodwin Sands." He jabbed a finger at the table. "Thirteen men-o'-war went aground that day. All were lost. Every man was lost."

"Good Lord," said Father softly.

"Ye can hear their wailin' on the wind. Ye can hear it in the fog."

"And we have to go through that?" asked I.

"Laddie, ye skirt 'em." Captain Crowe put his finger on the lump of bread that he'd set down for the *Dragon*. He slid it out, among the crumbs; he snaked it down a twisting path. "Ye tak' the long road out, ye see. Ye've got the lead swinging, and ye luff her up, ye turn and come about." His finger twisted through the crumbs, and I watched it as though if it ever touched a single bit of bread, we would all be on the instant drowned. "Slowly, slowly," said Captain Crowe. "In and out, touch and go." Then his finger reached the open surface of the table, and I heard Father release his breath, and I realized that I'd been holding mine as well. We both laughed. And so did Captain Crowe.

"Och, it's no as bad as that," said he, and swept the table bare of crumbs. "No harder than crossing this room, if you know the waters as well as I do."

"I need to find a man like that," said Father.

"Aye, ye do." The captain tightened his cloak. "Believe me, ye do. I've crossed those sands in winter gales and summer fog, and there's few can say the same. Och, right enough ye have to find someone. Now, who might that be?" He stroked his chin, as though the question puzzled him. But I saw his eyes, and in them an eagerness, barely concealed, to be off on the *Dragon* himself.

Father didn't see the dark glimmer there. He had his head down, working at his bread and soup. But suddenly he looked up. And, smiling, he thumped his forehead with his fist. "Damn my eyes!" he shouted. "He's sitting right in front of me."

"Where?" said Captain Crowe. He swung himself around to stare off into the dark shadows of the inn.

"Here," said Father, laughing. "You. Captain Crowe, will you take the *Dragon* across the Sands?"

"Me? The *Dragon*?" he asked. Slowly he came back to face Father. He wore an expression of amazement, but one so transparent he might have painted it on. "I suppose I could at that," he said. "Aye, why not indeed?"

"Splendid," Father said. "You can come with us in the morning and have a look at the boat."

"Ha'd your wheest!" the captain cried. "I canna be off as quickly as that. I've business to see to."

"Business?" said Father.

"Affairs," said he. "When ye've bought the ship ye can send for me. I'll need three days, and then I'll come doon on the coach." He smiled. "It's the best I can dae."

"Fair enough," said Father. He rubbed his palms together, then closed them with a slap. "And now, will you share a glass? We can lay our plans together."

"Why not?" said the captain, grinning. "I'll even stand ye a round, Mr. Spencer. And we'll drink to a voyage together."

He heaved himself up and went at a rolling seaman's gait from table to table down the length of the parlor. The moment he was gone I leaned toward Father. "You played right to his hand," said I. "Didn't you see it was just what he wanted?"

"Oh, John," said Father. "Of *course* I did. The man's a devil, but a harmless one. Proud as Punch, and that's his failing. Too blasted proud to come straight out and ask for something. But he's just the one for the job, don't you agree?"

I shrugged.

"Well?" said Father.

"You don't know him," I said. "And you're going to hire him as the captain?"

"Good heavens, no," said Father. "As *pilot*, John. Only as pilot. You don't think he imagines he's going as the captain, do you?"

But he did. Crowe came back with three glasses nested in his fists. He set a large one before Father and said with a laugh, "One for the owner." Then, "One for the boy," said he, and set a small glass at my elbow. Last he hoisted his own, an enormous pot full of ale. "And one for the captain," he said.

Father groaned. "You misunderstand me, my friend. I

have a captain already, and a good one. But you've put a scare into me, and I'd like you to go along and see the *Dragon* over the Sands."

The captain, still on his feet, glowered down. I saw his fingers tighten round the glass. "Turner Crowe," he said proudly, "doesna sail as crew."

"Then Turner Crowe stays ashore," said Father.

I feared the glass might shatter in the captain's hand, so hard did he squeeze. It shook in his fist, and his eyes had become slits. Such a sudden flash of rage I had seldom seen, and I imagined the man could be a horror on a ship of his own. Plainly he was used to *giving* the orders, not getting them.

"So what will it be?" asked Father.

"I'd hate to see a fine ship lost," said Crowe, "and men like yourselves go with her." Anger gave an edge to his voice and made his words sound threatening. But he lowered his head in a humble way, and his eyes went down to the table. "Aye, I'll be yer pilot, Mr. Spencer. I'll see her safe across the Sands."

"Splendid," said Father. Even I was pleased at this. After the dire warnings that Larson had thrust upon us, it was good to find a man who knew the ship and trusted her.

He dropped to his chair. Its legs creaked under him. "Who *is* the captain, then?" he asked. "Like as not, I've shipped wi' him before."

"Dawson," said Father. "Do you know him?"

"Aye," said Crowe. "He's a tall man, dark of hair."

"He's short and fair," said Father.

"Bearded, is he not? With a London accent?"

"Liverpool," said Father. "And he's clean-shaven."

"Och, aye," said Crowe. "I know him well."

Father glanced at me. He found amusement in the man's clumsy maneuvers and showed it with a wink. "The two of you will have a lot to talk about," said he.

Crowe nodded. But his thoughts, I saw, had wandered off to somewhere else. His eyes were dark.

"You'll see Dawson at the River Stour," said Father. "He's leaving London tomorrow. He'll put up for the night at Canterbury, and go direct to the *Dragon* from there."

Crowe lifted his head. He was smiling now, all hint of anger gone. "I'll look forward to seeing him," he said. "Aye, a pleasure it will be."

Father drained his glass. "One more?" he asked. "I've got a lot to tell you, Captain Crowe."

I was sent off to look for Mrs. Pye. I took a lamp and went from the dim glow of the parlor to the darkness of the hallway. The light went before me, leaping over plastered walls, turning doorways from black to gold as I came toward them. I heard Mrs. Pye long before I saw her.

"Fleming?" she asked. "Is that you?"

With a suddenness that startled me, she stepped up from a staircase, from a blackness below, into the gleam of my lamp. She reached for my arm, and her hands were bitterly cold as she touched my shoulder, then my cheek. I saw the disappointment on her face when she found I wasn't Fleming.

"Who's this?" she asked.

"John Spencer," I said. "My father sent me to find you. He and the captain want another glass."

Her hands dropped away, and she carried on and past me, back the way I'd come. I went with her, and the shadows followed. But as they thickened in around the staircase I saw—or thought I did—a faint veil of light, as though from a lantern down at the foot of the stairs. For a moment I smelled the saltiness of the sea, carried up from below on a cold draft of air. But just as quickly it vanished again, and the glow of light went with it.

Chapter 4
THE *DRAGON*

At dawn the next day I collected our two small bags, and we left the Baskerville Inn. Captain Crowe came out to the door, pointing down the road to give us our directions.

"Ye've near a mile to walk," said he. "And ye'll have to hurry now, if ye've a mind to catch the coach."

I was surprised to find that we were so far from the sea as we walked along a road that took us to the edge of cliffs before curving inland to the west. The inn stood well above the water, fully half a mile from the nearest line of surf. I couldn't understand how I had smelled the salt air so strongly from there on a night without any wind.

Father was back to his old self, striding along with his cane swinging at his arm, barely limping at all. He had only the one coat, but underneath he wore a good, clean shirt, and I could see the whiteness of it through the hole from the highwayman's pistol. It flashed across his chest like a medal he had won.

All the way to St. Vincent, and all the way north in the coach to Pegwell Bay, he talked of Captain Crowe.

"The man has been around the Horn," he said. "He's been to the Indies, East *and* West. Yet there he sat at the Baskerville. What were the chances of that?"

I thought the chances were rather good that the man would be found wherever there was liquor, but I didn't tell Father that. And we rode to the north with the sea at our right as the dust clouded round the carriage.

It was evening before we arrived and I saw the *Dragon* for the first time. She lay in the incoming tide, with her stern facing us, and I thought she was just about the prettiest little ship I'd ever seen. Though smaller by half than our old *Isle of Skye*, she looked clever and quick. With her sails carefully furled on the booms and the big yards of the topsail set perfectly square, she looked more like a small warship than a merchantman.

"So it's still for sale," said Father, staring up at the masthead. I followed his gaze and saw the broom lashed there, a signal to all that a buyer was wanted.

"That's good," said he. "Providence is with us, young John."

Right away we hired a boat to take us out to the *Dragon*. The oarsman had only one arm, and so he sculled instead of rowed, standing at the stern, grunting with each heave of the oar. "Sit still!" he snapped at me as I scrambled forward into the bow. "It's hard enough to move this old bit of rot without you flopping around like a herring."

Father's eyes snapped wide. He was facing forward, and he said over his shoulder, "I'd thank you to keep a civil tongue in your head."

"And I'd thank you to keep a silent one in yours," said the oarsman. "You'd think you might come on the ebbing tide. But no. Lord, no. You're from London, you are, and what's it to you if I have to do twice the work?" He was the rudest boatman I'd ever met.

Father gritted his teeth. "Just take us around the front of the boat."

"The front of the boat!" said the sculler with a sneer. "Lord save me from landsmen. You mean the pointed end, do you?" He pulled and pushed on the oar, the empty sleeve flapping at his side. "I'll take you round the *bow*, I think. Round the *bow* of that *schooner*. Twice the distance, but what's it to you?"

The oar squealed in its notch in the transom as we snaked forward, twisting through the water. Slowly the ship grew larger, until she was all that I could see. We went up her long, black side, up toward the bowsprit. And there, below it, crouched a dragon.

This was Father's "enormous great figurehead." A wooden dragon, its mouth agape and lined with teeth, it stared ferociously toward the open sea. Its lower jaw was fully half a fathom above the water, the mouth so wide that I could have crawled inside it. The eyes were yellow, and they seemed to glow, and the reflections of the water danced across them. It gave the dragon an evil glint, and its big flared nostrils almost seemed to breathe out smoke and fire.

We passed right below it, between the mouth and the thick cable of the anchor. I turned my head to see the face, and the dragon seemed to watch me.

"What do you think?" asked Father. He sounded so proud, he might have carved it himself.

"It's wonderful," said I.

"It's madness," the boatman said. "It's something a Frenchman would do."

"Was it built by the French?" asked Father.

"Don't you know even *that*? Good crikey! The *Dragon* was built here in Kent to fight against the French. Only later did she fight against England."

"She's got no guns," said I. "No gunports."

"There's other ways to fight," the boatman said. "The Froggies used her to bring their spies across the Channel. She smuggled spies to England."

The boatman brought us beyond the *Dragon*, then let the tide swing us round to face her. In silence we floated on the river, drifting down toward her, all of us staring at that huge and frightful head. Then Father cracked his fist against the gunwale. "I'm going to buy it," he said. "By the saints, I'm going to buy that boat!"

"You've lost your head." The boatman swore. "She'll bring you trouble and nothing else. See how black she is? It's her soul you're looking at. Her heart is black inside her."

"That's rubbish," said Father.

"I think not." With a sweep of his oar, the boatman brought us in toward the hull. "Half her life she's been a smuggler. First from France and then from England. And it spoils her, mark my words. Once a ship has seen a smuggling run, she's spoiled for anything else."

Father stood up. He nearly lost his balance, then found it, and reached out with his cane to hook on to the *Dragon*'s shrouds.

I went up after Father, and the boatman drifted down the hull. He neither came aboard nor even touched the ship.

"Wait here," said Father.

"Not on your life," said the boatman as the tide took him away. "You want me, you whistle. I ain't laying here beside her." He shouted after us even as he vanished on the tide. "I don't trust her, I don't."

When he was just a tiny thing, turning in the current, he still called across the water. "She'll seek out dangers. For the sake of the boy, find another ship."

Had Father listened, I would only have talked him out of it. The *Dragon* was a lovely thing, and I could hardly wait to sail. We looked her over from bow to stern, from deck to keelson. Father paced through the holds, counting his steps, converting the total into barrels and boxes and bags.

"It's smaller than it looks from the outside," said he. "But the boat can pay its way, I've no doubt of that."

We walked through the cabins, from large to small, forward from the stern. In the last, Father could stretch his hands from side to side. "This one will be yours," he said.

"Mine?" said I.

"You'll be the owner's representative." He sat on the narrow bunk. He wrote with an imaginary quill on imaginary ledgers spread across the table. "You'll be second to none but the captain."

31

I stood with my head bowed; the cabin was too low to stand upright. "Father, I would rather be a sailor. Just an ordinary sailor."

"Just a mindless slug?" he asked. "Just a pair of hands, is all?" He looked at me and smiled. "Oh, you'll get your share of work. You'll be at the wheel and up the mast and tangled in the ropes, I'm sure. But you'll have to see to the business as well."

"The business?" I asked.

"The manifests," said he. "The cargo. The food and water, the sailcloth and whatnot." He made a rolling motion with his hand, like a wheel going on and on. "But work hard, study well, and you'll be a captain yourself before you know it."

I was pleased with this, though I would have agreed to anything for a chance to sail on the *Dragon*.

Father went back to London, and I stayed at a waterfront inn. I expected Captain Dawson to arrive, but the days went by and he didn't. I passed my time walking on the fishermen's wharves or sitting for hours on the riverbank, just staring at that graceful ship. And nearly a week was out before a letter came from Father.

My dearest son,

A tragedy has befallen us. Poor Captain Dawson was overtaken by thieves on his way from London and was killed in Canterbury as he waited for the coach. I know you share my grief at this, but we must buck up and carry on.

I have sent word to Captain Crowe at the Basker-

ville, who may already, as you receive this, be on the road to Pegwell Bay. I have asked him to assume command, and he has replied in a favorable way. You will understand that the state of affairs is such that I will not be able to come and see you off on this first voyage of the _Dragon._ And so, with the greatest of confidence, I am entrusting to you the duties of loading a cargo of wool and bringing it to our docks in London. Enclosed are various papers attesting to legal ownership of the _Dragon,_ and others setting forth the particulars of the cargo, including details of from where and from whom it is to be obtained. You will answer to Captain Crowe in all matters pertaining to the sailing of the boat, but as to the welfare of the cargo and its expediency in delivery—matters of safety notwithstanding—he shall be subservient to yourself. I have spelled this out to him, and trust there will be no difficulties.

You will sail as soon as the cargo is loaded, and you will come directly to London. Considering the vagaries of wind and weather, I will not worry unduly until a fortnight has passed from this date.

I am, in closing, your most loving and respectful

Father

I moved aboard the _Dragon_ that very day, and though it shames me to say it, I frolicked like a child in a ship that was all my own. I ran shouting through the cabins and the hold; I skylarked in the rigging. I clattered pots and juggled with belaying pins. I climbed to the mainmast head and cut away the broom that marked her as a ship for sale. I climbed to the foremast, and I inched along the footropes of the long and slender topsail yard. I was hanging upside down from the ratlines, singing the only chantey I knew, when I heard a shout below me and saw Captain Crowe staring up from the afterdeck.

"When ye're through wi' that," he said, "I should like a word wi' ye, Mr. Spencer."

No man had ever called me that, and I blushed as red as roses. The one-armed man, just sculling off toward the shore, gave me a cheeky grin. "Box his ears, Cap'n," he told Turner Crowe. "It's what I would do, the scallywag. And box 'em for me while you're at it."

Captain Crowe had a great heap of things piled beside the rail: two chests, a duffel, a pair of boots stuffed to their tops with rolled-up signal flags. Across his shoulders was the same cloak of salt-stained cloth, and tucked inside it, below his arm, he carried a bulky roll of charts. And with these, as I came up to him, he struck me lightly on the head.

"Dignity," said he, and smiled. "Ye should a'ways act as if there's someone there to watch ye."

"Yes, sir," I said.

His face was ruddy and all aglow, the eyes lost within their wrinkles. He said, "Have ye seen to the cargo?"

"No, sir," I said.

"Have ye seen to a berth?"

"No," said I.

He shook his head. "Then we'd best get started. There's muckle work to be done."

Chapter 5
THE CREW
COMES ABOARD

Captain Crowe might have been a different man from the one I had found at the Baskerville Inn. Sober as a rock, cheerful to a fault, he went to work with a fever that shamed me for ever doubting him. Before a day had passed, the *Dragon* was moored alongside a jetty and the cargo of wool was coming aboard. Enormous bales arrived, and a swarm of men carried them up, each bent under his awkward load. They staggered up one plank and scampered down another, a long line going round and round, making me think of ants at a sugar bowl. Slowly the holds came full.

I stood with my lists, now and then taking them into my mouth to haul on a line and help a barrel or box aboard. I worked from sunup to sundown, until my head reeled with figures; I dreamt of numbers in my sleep that night.

Captain Crowe was here, there, and everywhere. He did a great deal of fussing down in the holds, a great deal of shouting up on the deck. At one point he took me aside and asked me to sit by the starboard rail.

He'd cast off his cloak, replacing it with a big cravat that hid his neck from shoulders to ears. His face, so reddened by the wind, seemed to bulge from it, as though he'd tied the cloth too tightly.

"Ye're doing well, Mr. Spencer," he said. "Your father would be proud to see ye."

"Thank you," said I.

"But there's the matter of—" He started, then stopped, and finally just laid it out. "Och, we havena got a crew."

So I had failed after all. I had somehow assumed that the crew would simply be there—though how or why, I couldn't imagine. With a sigh, I got out my lists and spread them on the deck. "How many do we need?"

He scratched his head. "A handful is plenty. A man and a boy can handle a schooner, Mr. Spencer. But I would think, say, three's a nice number."

I wrote that down, then said, "How do I find them?"

"Och, ye've been put over your head," said he, and smiled in a kindly manner. "I'll tell ye, John. The usual way is that ye ask the captain to do it."

This I knew was not true. Finding the hands who'd work a ship was a task that Father would never have left to the captain. Yet neither had he assigned it to me.

"But o' course," said Crowe, seeing my hesitation, "if ye'd rather tak' it upon yoursel' . . ." He shrugged and started to go. "No matter to me. I was only trying to dae ye a wee kindness."

This he said gruffly, with that same edge of anger I'd heard at the Baskerville, as though he'd taken offense at my doubts. I watched him lumber off, and I remembered what Father had said: *"The man's a devil, but a harmless one. Proud as Punch, and that's his failing."*

"Wait," I called after him. He turned back to face me. "I would like that, Captain Crowe, if you'd do that favor for me."

"Aye, aye," he said, and smiled. But his smile was a troubling one, one that reminded me how thin was my thread of authority. Only that thread, I saw, kept him from giving me the back of his hand instead of his kindness.

But Crowe took up the task with great efficiency, and in a single trip to shore he found a crew for the *Dragon*. It was as though the men were there and waiting, so quickly did they come aboard. Captain Crowe brought them up the plank like sheep that he was herding. He put them straight to work lashing down the hatches.

"Three good men," he told me. "Twa to reef and steer, anither to dae the cooking and the whatnot. There's only one I canna vouch for. But I hear he's good at his work, with eyes like a hawk in the dark."

Why this was a virtue, I didn't bother asking. It was enough for me simply to have them aboard. They seemed neither young nor old, just three sailors, one long and thin, one as broad as an ox. And the third wore a thing so bulky and huge that he could scarcely get his arms in front of him to tighten up his knots. Curious, I walked up to him and saw that it was a strange sort of jerkin he wore, every inch of it covered with corks that he must have sewn in place one at a time, in layers and layers. It reminded me of nothing less than a huge and hollow pinecone.

He looked up from his work with the widest grin I'd ever seen. "And here he is," said he. "Here's the boy that tamed the Haggis."

"The what?" I asked.

"The Haggis! Captain Crowe," he said. "The man's a bloated old gut stuffed full of pudding and blood. But I've never seen the old gaffer so meek, bobbing like a pigeon, hopping to your orders." He pecked with his nose at the air, so comical an imitation that I threw back my head and laughed.

He was pleased with his cleverness. "You'll get along fine, I think," said he. "But don't cross him, you hear? Oh, he gets in a fit when he's mad."

"I've seen that already," I said.

"And you'll see it again if he catches you here." The corks squeaked against each other as he stretched to look past me. Then he spoke in a warbling Scottish brogue, a mockery of the captain: "Aff ye go, ye sleekit beastie!"

I returned to my lists as the sailors finished their lashings and went on to work at the sails. And when the captain came up from below, I stopped him at the mainmast.

"Captain Crowe?" said I, pointing to the sailors. "Who is that man?"

"Eh?" he asked. "Which man's that?"

"The one with all the corks."

"Och, that's only Tommy Dusker." The captain laughed. "They call him Dasher."

It was a good name for him. His hair was loose and flowing, not tarred in the usual fashion. He had a thin little mustache, side-whiskers, and teeth that sparkled like polished stones. He moved his legs with graceful ease, yet from the waist up he was ungainly as an elephant.

"I've sailed wi' him before," said Captain Crowe. "He's a good man."

"Why does he wear those corks?"

"Dasher's afraid of the water," said Crowe.

I couldn't believe it. "A sailor afraid of the water?"

"Aye. It's odd, isn't it?"

That was all he would say. Suddenly there was a task that needed his attention, and I didn't see him again until evening, when the *Dragon* was ready to sail.

We took the lashings from the sails, and hauled aloft the canvas. With creaks and groans the *Dragon* came to life, as though the sails were wings she spread, on bony spars stretched toward the clouds. The wind became her breath, and she sighed as she started down the river, free from land at last. She shivered with her eagerness to get upon the sea.

The setting sun behind us, we rode the tide past wharves and warehouses, past the landsmen who stopped and stood to watch us go. But the wind was faint, and it vanished with the sun. And when the tide, turning to the flood, threatened to carry us back again, we dropped our anchor in the Downs to wait for wind and weather.

I stood on the afterdeck and watched the sea go dark. Well to the west, I noticed whitecaps where there was no wind. When Captain Crowe came up, a wooden box in his hand, I pointed to the surf and asked him what it meant.

"That's the Goodwin Sands," said he, with only the briefest of glances. "It's the tide running over the Sands that ye're seeing."

I leaned on the rail and stared at the water as it surged and broke. Then humps appeared, some dark, some shining where the last of the sun touched the sand. They looked like the backs of enormous serpents, and I found it strange to think they were moving even now, as though alive, shifting with the tide. I thought of the thirteen ships that had gone aground, the hundreds of men who had been lost. And, in the twilight, I heard their wailing.

It started faintly at first, then rose to an awful screech—a keening and a droning that sent shivers up my back. But when I turned around, I laughed.

Captain Crowe had his bagpipes out. The wooden box was empty on the deck, and in his arms he held this thing, like a streamered, five-horned beast he was killing in his hands. His eyes for once were wide, his cheeks puffed out, his face the brightest red. He started walking with the pipes, and the wailing turned to a tune.

The crew came up from the fo'c's'le and sat in a knot by the capstan. Dasher was in the middle, looking as fat as a carnival man in his strange suit of corks. I saw the flare of tinder sparks, and then the cheerful glow of pipe bowls. Crowe's music rose through the rigging and swirled across the sea. It was sad music that filled me with a yearning to be among the men at the bow, just a sailor and nothing more.

The tune ended and another began. It was fast and merry, and Dasher stood up to dance. His hands at his hips, now at his back, he jigged upon the capstan. He leapt and twirled, he kicked his legs, and the others clapped to see him. He was at once graceful and grotesque.

I wondered if Dasher had always been afraid of the sea. Down the length of the ship, he was just a bobbing figure who seemed to feel only joy at the prospect of our adventure. Yes, the *Dragon* was a happy ship, I thought, and the voyage would be all too short. But on both accounts I was wrong.

In the morning we sat becalmed. The sun was huge and bright, and there was not a breath of wind. Yet out beyond the Sands I saw the sails of trading ships and frigates scuttling to and fro. Some were making for the river, yet they came pressed by a breeze that did not reach us.

"What's wrong with the wind?" I asked the captain. "Do you think you could whistle one up?"

"Och, it's no the wind," said Crowe. "It's the *Dragon.*" He touched her rail with his hand. "She's waiting on something, I think. She's biding her time, ye see."

Through a long afternoon the ships came into the Downs. The wind chased them in and left them there, sails hanging slack from the yards. In a flock, they rode the tide as far as they could, then anchored when it turned against them. And in the evening there was a ring of ships around us, all of them waiting, every one of them lying head to the tide, patient as sheep in a pasture.

I took my supper alone, in a seat still warm from another's body, in the sound of laughter from the fo'c's'le. The food was cold, my dish speckled with the dried lumps of someone else's dinner, and I went rather dolefully to my cramped little quarters at the bow of the schooner, thinking I might write a note to my father.

I gathered my paper, pen, and bottle of ink and started up to the deck to sit in the evening sun. But I never finished the journey.

At the end of the corridor the captain's door stood ajar. And through the gap I saw him there, seated on his bunk and staring at the porthole. His fingers touched at the *Dragon*'s hull, stroking the curve of a massive rib. And though I could see that no one else was there, Captain Crowe was talking. His voice was far too soft to let me hear the words, but he wasn't praying, I was sure of that. He wasn't talking to himself. All I could imagine was that he was talking to the ship.

Seeing him there, hearing the murmur of his voice, made me think of a time when I was young, when my mother became ill and took to what would be her deathbed. Father would go to her and close the door, and I would hear him talking in that same sad voice that came to me now through the captain's door.

I didn't disturb the man. I went back to my cabin and penned my little note as the tide burbled past the planking at my elbow. Then Captain Crowe went clomping up on deck, and soon after, I put down my quill and followed him.

The sun was setting over Kent. The captain's shadow warped across the deck as he fiddled with his wooden box, taking out his bagpipes. The shadow lengthened when he stood, and spiked with the shape of his drones.

At the first sound of the pipes, the crew came to sit at the capstan, and it was as though the day had not existed at all.

Soon Dasher was dancing, his wild hair flying, his corks bouncing. And I stood by myself at the rail as the captain paced, as the crew laughed and clapped and smoked. To see it made me lonesome, and, thinking I might join the men, I started forward, past the mainmast, past the cabin. But when I reached the foremast, one of them looked up. There was a nudging of elbows, and all as one the trio went below, down to the gloom of the fo'c's'le. The last was Dasher, who had to jam himself through the hatchway.

The music stopped then, and Captain Crowe called out to me, down half the length of the *Dragon*. "Mr. Spencer, come aft, if ye please."

The bagpipes were still under his arm, the long horns of the drones hanging down. The bag wheezed softly, as though he had almost—but not quite—strangled the life out of it.

"Ye're not one o' the crew," he said. There was no anger in his voice, and he turned as I came up, to walk beside me along the rail. "Ye'll find it's a lonely life sometimes, being a part o' the afterguard. But good or bad, that's the way it is."

"Yes, sir," I said. I knew the cook was called Harry and that he was the biggest of the three, a dim-looking man with arms as thick as my legs. And the thin pole of a man was called Mathew, but that was all I knew. I had spoken only once with Dasher, and not at all with either of the others.

"Ye'll get used to it. Ye'll get to like it, even." With each step the captain took, the bagpipes groaned beneath his arm. "When the *Dragon* thinks the time has come, we'll make our offing. Then a quick call at t'other place, and it's on to London. More or less."

"What other place?" I asked.

Captain Crowe stopped walking. "Didn't your father tell you, then?"

"Tell me what?"

He frowned. "Och, the man was affy busy."

Captain Crowe knelt on the deck. He put his bagpipes down and stretched them along his wooden box. "We've got another cargo waiting for us. We're to pick it up and . . ." He shook his head. "Yer father should have telt ye this. We're to fill the holds—"

"No," said I. "That isn't right."

"Aye, it is," he insisted. The bagpipes squealed and shouted as he shoved them in the box. "Living on the *Dragon* the way ye were, I suppose ye never got his orders."

"But I wasn't on the *Dragon* at first," I said. "I stayed at an inn, and he sent me instructions there." I felt through my pockets, searching for the letter.

"Och, those are the old orders." He closed the box; he snapped the latches shut. "The new orders came to the Baskerville. And they say what I'm telling ye now."

Crowe came to his feet, and he was taller than me by only inches. Yet for a moment I felt almost fearful, for I heard in his voice that old hint of anger. *"Don't cross him,"* Dasher had said.

But he didn't get angry. He sighed, and smiled, and said, "But o' course, it's no for me to say. If ye want to tak' this wool to London, Mr. Spencer, then who am I to argue?" He gazed toward the masthead, and his fingers stroked his chin. "It isna me who'll have to answer to your father."

I stared at him and wondered what I should do. Had

Father, in his rush, changed his plans and then forgotten to tell me? Or had he sent a second letter that never reached me on the *Dragon*?

It was past all understanding. Maybe Captain Crowe had the old orders and *I* the new ones. No matter what I did, I might turn up in London with the wrong cargo. And through my foolishness, Father might lose a fortune.

I carried these thoughts up and down the deck. I felt them weighing upon me as though they were bricks instead of mere ideas. I almost wished that Captain Crowe would *order* me to take this new direction.

But he only stood and watched me pace. Now and then he asked, "Well?" or "What's it going to be?"

But in the end, the choice was neither mine nor his to make. For a message came, carried on the river, borne by a thing that would forever give me nightmares.

Chapter 6
AN EERIE WIND

It was just a speck in the falling tide, a dot of black floating in the river. It came out of a mist that hugged the land, out from the night to the dawn.

It was I who saw it first; I thought it was a coconut. And I watched it curiously, to see if it might pass close beside us. Then suddenly I saw the arms, just below the water, the fingers white as pastry. They were moving, but barely so, like the tentacles of a jellyfish. The speck was a head, and it turned from black to white as the face lifted up, and then to black again as all but his hair disappeared. Startled, I called for Captain Crowe.

He came up half dressed, his clothes awry, fastening first the big cravat around his neck. He took a glance down to the water, then led me to the bows, and we stood above the great carved dragon as the tide rippled past below us.

"Ah," said Captain Crowe. "This will be what the old *Dragon*'s been a-waiting for."

The man came weaving on the current. First to the left, then to the right, but always toward the *Dragon.* He came around the stern of an anchored ship, around the bow of another. Then he bumped against the dragon's mouth, and his arms spread wide across the wood, as though he meant to hold it. He floated there, on his stomach, his face within the water.

"He's dying," I said.

"He's dead already," said Captain Crowe. "But we'd better bring him up. It seems he's come to find us."

Mathew scrambled up and rigged a tackle from the forestay. I went down, right to the very mouth of the wooden dragon, and held the man by the collar. His hand swirled away from the hull and brushed against my wrist. His touch was so cold, so clammy, that I knew I held a dead man. Then my skin revolted at the thought of this, and I shook so badly that his head bobbed up and down. But a bight of rope was lowered for me, and I passed it around his shoulders. "Haul away," I said, and climbed to the deck.

The sailors pulled, the corpse came up; they pulled again, and he rose some more. He seemed to dance and shake, climbing from the water like a puppet from a stage. His chin rested on his chest, and his hair hung down to hide his face. And then he dangled above the rail, a figure in gray with buckled shoes, and the water fell from him in splashes on the deck.

"Och, he's a wee manny," said Captain Crowe. "Just a wee little manny." He reached out and lifted the chin and I gasped.

"Larson," I said. The gentleman from the carriage. He

had promised to find me, I remembered. He had told me to watch for him. *"I think I'm a dead man,"* he'd said. *"Now or later, I'm a goner."*

"You know him, then?" asked Captain Crowe.

"I met him once," said I.

Then Dasher spoke behind me. He said, "Throw him back." He laughed, and I thought I'd heard that laugh before. "He seems to like his swimming," Dasher said. "He's doing so well at it, he might be in Devon in a day or two."

"Stow it!" roared Captain Crowe. It was the first time in two days I'd heard him shout. "We'll heave him aboard, and when we're out at sea we'll bury him." He saw me watching, and he tried to smile. "A proper burial," he added.

Poor little Larson was swung inboard and lowered to the deck. And the instant his shoes touched the planks, the wind came up. It wasn't strong, but it was fair. It carried a smell of muddy earth, in a strange and chilling coldness, and the *Dragon* tugged against her anchor like a horse against its harness.

"Make sail!" said Captain Crowe. He was grinning, his crinkled eyes barely there. "Main and foresail, jib and staysail. Lively, lads; the *Dragon* wants to go."

Larson was left in a slump at the rail, the bight of rope still around his shoulders. Mathew and Harry went to the halyards, the captain to the sail lashings.

"Mr. Spencer, you'll tak' the wheel, if ye please," said Crowe. "We'll go south to the end of the Sands."

Huge and white, the sails streamed up and opened, flapping in the breeze. The anchor came aboard, and I felt us drifting back across the Downs. I spun the wheel; the

Dragon lurched on her side. I spun it the other way, and she turned her head toward the open sea.

It was an eerie wind that the dead man brought. It touched the *Dragon* but no other ship, and we passed through the anchored fleet like a silent, drifting cloud. A rippling patch of water went with us, but all around was calm. We sailed on a reach past a big East Indiaman that sat so still, even her flag wasn't ruffled. On every ship, a line of astonished men watched us pass.

"Set the topsail," said Captain Crowe, and—still grinning—he opened his long wooden box. "I'll even pipe ye aloft."

And so the *Dragon* went to sea, with a skirl of pipes in a ghostly breeze. The drifting dunes of the Goodwin Sands went by to port, the shores of Kent to starboard, and I alone steered this ship, this little world of ours. The square topsail flapped and filled, and I felt the pulse of the *Dragon* through the wheel as she quickened on her way.

But soon Dasher came to take my place. "You can go," he said. "I'll steer this thing. What's the course?"

"Running free," said I.

"Running free," he answered with a nod. "Straight ahead. Steady as she goes." He wore an impish grin. "Lord love me, I like this sailor talk."

He settled in behind the wheel, his arms poking out from his suit of corks as though from a barrel, awkwardly bent to grasp the spokes.

Suddenly he seemed disturbingly familiar. His laughter, his swaggering walk, even the words that he sometimes used made me think of the highwayman who had stopped us in the forest. But I could see that he knew what he was doing when it came to working a ship. He looked up at the sails, then down at the compass, and with the smallest turn of the wheel he gained half a knot. The wake stretched arrow-straight behind the *Dragon*'s stern.

"You can go," he said again. "They're about to launch that little gent. That fancy friend of yours."

"A little fancy gent," the highwayman had called him. I watched Dasher as he steered the ship. I said, "Have you seen that man before?"

"Don't ask me that," he said, and laughed. "I'm a terrible one for faces. Even worse for names. I pass my very own mother on the street and think, 'Now, who's that Mrs. Hickenbothom?' Get along now or you'll miss the launching. The Haggis wants your help."

Up at the bows, Captain Crowe had a swath of sailcloth spread across the fo'c's'le deck. He was down on his hands and knees, cutting out a burial shroud. His knife ripped through the cloth, and he went along behind it. At the pinrail on the weather side, Mathew and the cook were coiling halyards. Side by side, they worked with their heads down, but now and then they lifted them, and I saw the worried looks they cast across the deck.

"Ah, Mr. Spencer," said Crowe. "Perhaps ye'll lend a hand."

We spread out the shroud and laid Larson upon it; we lifted him there, with the captain at his heels and me at his head. He made a sorry sight, his tiny hands and face all ghastly pale. His eyes were not quite closed; his mouth hung open. I said, "We need a cloth. A tie to put around his head."

"Och," said Crowe, "we'll just wrap him in the shroud."

"No," said I. "I'd like to do it right."

He tore a piece of cloth into a ribbon, which he gave to me. I tied it round the dead man's chin, and when I lifted his head I discovered that the bones were all broken. I felt them grinding in my fingers.

"He didn't drown," I said, looking up at Captain Crowe. "Someone smashed his skull."

The captain came and prodded Larson's head. "Aye, ye might be right. Or he might have had a fall."

"Whatever happened," I said, "it wasn't long ago." There was still a pinkish touch of blood in his mat of hair. "He was alive when he set out for the *Dragon*."

Crowe shrugged. He squinted at me. "Still, we canna keep him on the ship. Ye dinna want to keep him, do ye?"

"No," I said. To have a corpse on board was the worst of luck. "But we should tell someone about it."

"Oh, aye," he said. "We'll do that, Mr. Spencer."

We folded the shroud over the body. The captain worked up from the feet, tucking and smoothing. Harry and Mathew crossed to the starboard pinrail, circling wide around the corpse, like cats past a sleeping dog. They went to work just yards away.

I didn't want to be the one to cover Larson's face; I started at his chest. And my hands, as they pressed and tugged at the cloth, felt a bulk below it, a square thing hard and stiff.

"There's something in his pockets," I said.

"I dinna see how that could be," said Crowe. "Dasher had a look already. Aye, and Mathew too. Didn't ye, Mathew?"

The sailor nodded, a quick and rapid gesture. He had prominent teeth, and the way his head moved made me think of a rabbit.

Captain Crowe grunted when I opened the shroud. "Och, Mr. Spencer," said he, "I'd like to get this done then."

I felt across Larson's wet clothes and found the thing, not within a pocket, but sewn behind the lining. The cloth was water-soaked and frayed from wear; I tore it with my fingers. And out came a little bundle, an envelope of oilskin.

"Whit's that, then?" asked Captain Crowe.

I opened the flap, and water poured out. It flowed down the side of the dead man's shroud, a rivulet tinged blue with ink. It streamed across the deck, then up, then down as the *Dragon* rolled to the south around the Goodwin Sands. The big curve of the jib threw shadows across us, and the wind ruffled cold at the papers I pulled from the pouch.

The first was a map folded in four. It was crudely drawn, and the lines had smudged near the creases, but I saw the coast of Kent and the English Channel, the entrance to the Thames. It was much like the image Captain Crowe had drawn on the table of the Baskerville, but in two places were markings in the shape of an X, and some writing was blurred beyond reading.

The second paper was a letter, but it too was badly smeared. It tore nearly in two when I tried to open it.

"What does it say?" asked Captain Crowe.

I held it out to him, but he shook his head. "I canna read," he told me.

I flattened the page on the planks of the deck. My fingers were soon blue with ink, as the whole top third of the letter was an enormous smudge, and the rest not much better. But I read aloud the parts I could—a few words here and there.

". . . have come among the Burton gang . . ."

"The Burton gang!" said Captain Crowe.

". . . a small army . . . eighty men . . . smuggling spirits . . ."

"Och, that's enough," said Crowe. "It's a lot of prattle."

But I kept reading. ". . . time running out . . . I am attracting suspicion . . ." And the last sentence was nearly all in the clear. "A major run is planned for six nights after the moon is full; the contraband of sixty barrels to be brought across in the . . ."

"In the what?" asked Captain Crowe.

"It doesn't say," said I. The rest was fully smudged.

I looked up from the letter to see the captain with his knife in his fist. He had come toward me across the spread-out remnants of the sailcloth, and now—at its edge—he squinted at me. The sailors, too, had stopped their work. Harry stood before me and Mathew behind, and the three made a silent tableau as the deck heaved up on a swell.

"And whit do ye mak' o this?" Crowe asked. "It seems like a lot o' daftness to me."

"I think he came to find me," I said. "He was fleeing from this smuggling gang, and he needed my help to get to London, maybe. He knew about the *Dragon*."

"Och, ye're as daft as the wee manny." Crowe dug his knife into the cloth and tore away a long and narrow ribbon. This he carried back to the shrouded body, and he started binding the dead man's knees. "Put it a' back in his pockets, I say. Let him tak' his secrets to his grave."

There was one more thing inside the pouch: a small book—a sort of ledger. It was so sodden that I had to peel the pages open one by one, like the layers of an onion.

Mathew and Harry moved closer, bending forward to see the book. Mathew sucked air through his teeth. But Captain Crowe only glanced at me. "And whit's that?" he asked.

"I don't know," said I. It seemed to be a list, but the writing was small and blurred. It filled nearly half the book, and beyond it the pages were blank.

"This gang," said Crowe. "This Burton gang. Ye've heard o' them before?"

"Oh, yes," I said. It was one of the largest smuggling gangs in all of England. I remembered Father reading of it in *The Times,* ranting about the villainy. But we'd heard nothing at all of the Burton gang for perhaps a year or more.

I kept turning pages as the *Dragon* slid along in a hiss of water. Whole sections passed through my fingers in thick and gummy wads. A list of names, perhaps; nothing more than that. And I was about to close the book when, right at the back, I found a note that was not quite so blurred as all the rest.

"Look at this," I said.

In a different, fainter ink, Larson had recorded every

detail of a smuggling run. There were dates and times; there were signals to be made and answered. Everything was included but the name of the ship and the harbor she sailed from. I read it out, and the captain listened, frowning, as he bundled up the dead man's body.

"Captain Crowe," I said, "it's now!"

"What?" His face grew even greater wrinkles. "Speak sense," he told me.

"Look." I shoved the book toward him before I realized it would do no good. "The dates, the moon; this is happening now. This smuggling ship," I said, and tapped the pages. "She left for France this very morning."

"Och, whit good does that do ye, then?" asked Captain Crowe. "There must be a thousand craft setting sail today, frae a hundred ports o' call on a hundred leagues o' coastline." He shook his head. "Laddie, ye're looking for a needle in a haystack."

What he said was true, and it took the wind from my sails in an instant. The mysterious smuggler could have been anywhere at all from London round to Devon—still in port or far at sea. It could have been a full-rigged ship or a tiny fishing boat. A needle in a haystack? That would be child's play to find, compared to one unnamed craft in all of southeast England.

Captain Crowe came to his feet. He put a hand at the small of his back as he turned to me. "Ye're like a dithering bodach," he said. "Will ye help me here, or no?" Then he glowered at Mathew and Harry. "Shove off, the pair o' ye now," he barked. "I dinna care a hoot if the halyards are coiled; it's no a royal yacht that ye're on."

Larson, his ashen face still uncovered, his eyes still barely open, seemed to watch me from his shroud. As the *Dragon* sailed along and Dasher steered us south, the dead man's head rocked slowly side to side, as though he shook it at me sadly in its ragged strip of sailcloth.

It wasn't mere chance that had brought him to the *Dragon*. He had come to me for help, and I felt I owed him that. I picked up the map and the letter and leapt to my feet.

"Captain Crowe," I said, "set a course for France."

Chapter 7
A DREADFUL CURSE

"Por France, ye say?" Captain Crowe stared at me with a look of utter amazement. "For France?" he said again. "Did I hear ye right?"

"Isn't the *Dragon* as fast as any ship around?" I asked. "Couldn't we sail to France before the smugglers and get the brandy that's waiting for them? Couldn't we make the signal they would make?"

I opened the book and tapped the pages. "It's only a pair of flags. The blue peter and the yellow jack. We could hoist them ourselves, Captain Crowe."

It seemed his eyes might pop from his head. He looked at me in the same astounded way that a visitor to Bedlam would stare at the lunatics. And I heard the excitement in my voice, and blushed.

"It's foolish," I said. "Isn't it?"

"Foolish?" said he. "Not at a', lad."

The sun rolled out from behind the jib, and his shadow

leapt across the deck to tangle at my feet. "Aye, we'll go across," he said. "If we crowd on sail, there's nary a ship can match the *Dragon*. We'll fill her every inch wi' tubs o' brandy." He laughed out loud. "It's a bonny scheme," he said. "It's a bonny, bonny scheme."

"But then," I said, "it's straight to London. No matter what my father told you, I want to follow my own instructions."

A dark expression came over his face. I realized he was getting angry, very quickly. His fingers tightened into fists.

"So that's the lay o' the land, is it?" he said. "Ye sense a little profit here for yourself and your father."

"Wait," I said, "I—"

"Ye sail into London wi' sixty tubs o' spirits that cost ye not a farthing. Och, I see your game." He stepped toward me, so close I felt his breath upon my face. "Weel, I'm the master and ye're a boy, and ye'll do whit I say. Now gie me that." He snatched away the map and the letter. Then he looked at the book in my hands and snatched that too. He ripped from its back the pages I'd shown him, and crumpled in his fist all the details of the smuggling run. The rest of the book he hurled back at me. It struck my chest and fell to the deck.

"You don't understand." I bent down for the book, but Crowe put his foot on top of it.

"We'll go to France for the brandy," he said. "But we'll no be taking it up to London."

"I don't *want* to take it to London." I had to look up at him, feeling small and childish. "I want to take the brandy right where the smugglers would. To the cross on the map.

But I'll go ashore—or someone will—and we'll have the revenue waiting. A trap, Captain Crowe. I want to set a trap."

His face began to soften, and the redness swiftly left it, the way a bit of metal cools when it's taken from a forge. I pointed at Larson. "He had no one else to turn to; I have to do this. Or I have to try. And when it's done, I want to take the *Dragon* home." I stared up at Captain Crowe, and already he was smiling. "That's all I meant," I said.

"Weel, it's a' for ye to say, Mr. Spencer. Ye're the owner's son." At last he lifted his boot from the deck. And with a gesture that I was sure was meant to be kindly, he nudged the book toward me with his toe. "She's your own ship, more or less," he said. "And I'm just a lowly sailor."

I didn't know how to reply. A moment before, he was the master and I a boy. One moment he was livid with anger, and the next he was doing all he could to please me.

"It's best to take the proper course," he continued as he helped me up with a tug on my collar. His smile had become a grin. "And if good King George thinks it fit to say a little 'thank ye' wi' a purse full o' guineas, then it's a' the better. But it's no for that I'll do it."

He was a scoundrel, I thought. It was *just* for that he'd do it.

"And now," he said happily, "let's get your friend over the side."

I put the book back in the envelope and shoved it in my pocket. We went back to the dreary task of wrapping Larson in his shroud. But Captain Crowe seemed more cheerful than he ever had, as though a tremendous burden had been taken from him. He laughed, and he tweaked the dead man's cheek before he covered up that poor white face. Then the body lay between us like a big cocoon, and the captain sent me down to fetch a weight. "A ballast stone," he said. "And mind ye get one big enough."

I fetched a lantern and went right to the depths of the ship, where water, brown and fetid, slurped among the timbers. I went through the darkness in a circle of light, frightening cockroaches into shelter, hearing the groans and creaks of the hull as it worked. The places where I had to go were small and cramped, and I slithered through them as the lantern made the shadows zoom and tilt.

And someone came behind me.

When I stopped, he was silent. When I moved, so did he. I heard a faint creaking of wood as he crept up, closing the distance. He was quiet as a cat. And suddenly I felt a hand touch my shoulder. I cried out, startled, as he pushed me down against the hull.

"You're in danger, boy," said he.

I tried to lift myself, to turn and see him, but the sailor held me down.

"Watch yourself," he said. "There's one aboard who'll kill you."

"Who?"

For a moment I only heard him breathing. He said, "The one who seems least likely."

"But who?" I asked again.

He pressed harder on my shoulder. "He'll want the dead man's secrets. See you keep them safe."

"Who are you?" I asked.

"A man you never saw." And then the hand was gone.

I struggled around and raised my lantern. But the sailor had vanished so quickly there was nothing to see but shadows. It was as though he had never come at all. Yet somehow I could *feel* him in the damp air, and for a long, long time I stayed still, listening and watching. But only shadows moved; only wood and water made a sound. And finally I carried on, down toward the stern.

I made my way to the lazarette, to a gloomy place below the wheel, where the tiller—as big as a ceiling beam—shook and rattled as it swung to turn the rudder post. The steering lines were badly slack, and they squealed through the blocks with the sound of frightened pigs. It was there I found a pile of stones, worn smooth and round, and began to take one from the top.

The tiller swung; the lines creaked. I heard the rush of water and the squawking of the gulls. I thought of Dasher just a deck away, above me at the wheel. It didn't seem possible that he meant me any harm, but . . . *"The one who seems least likely."* I felt as though a dreadful curse had been placed upon me, that the man I would come to trust would be the one to harm me. But who? And why?

"He'll want the dead man's secrets."

With shaking hands and a racing heart, I took Larson's pouch from my pocket, and the little book from that.

I set the lantern on the deck and knelt beside it as it rocked on its bottom with a little tick of metal. I opened the book and turned it to catch the glow from the flame. Water had left the writing indistinct, but I could see that it held a list of names—of smugglers, I supposed. Some were blurred and others not, and all were copied by the water backward onto the page before. Here and there was one so clear that it leapt out at me: Richard Harks, miller; Gordon Burns, apothecary. Somewhere in the book would be a name I knew, but the list was set down in no order, and most entries I couldn't read at all. The lamp rocked beside me: *tick, tick, tick.*

Then, suddenly, it stopped. A grinding, groaning crack of wood echoed through the ship. I heard footsteps above me. Two people, or three; it was hard to tell. And suddenly the room tilted up and sent me flying across the deck.

I crashed against the hull and saw the lantern teeter on its side, then tumble down toward me. Glass shattered. Oil poured out. The wick flared and guttered. And I threw myself forward, smothering the tiny glow before the oil could catch and the whole ship go up in flames.

The tiller rumbled to the side and back; the lines that held it screamed. With a lurch, the deck came level.

I was left in almost utter darkness. Only tiny slits of light slipped past the cheeks of the rudder. And with them came the sound of the gulls, a screeching that unnerved me. Crouched in that space with the book in my hand, I was seized with a sudden fear that the man who meant me harm would find me with it there. I shoved the book, in its envelope, down among the ballast stones, deep within the pile. I took a stone into my shaking grasp and fumbled with it back the way I'd come.

Captain Crowe was waiting at the companionway. He took the stone, and I went behind him along the deck.

Dasher stood at the wheel, but I saw no sign of Mathew or Harry.

"Ye get lost down there?" asked Crowe over his shoulder.

"My lantern broke," I told him.

He grunted. "We touched the Sands. They're shifting, see."

He worked the stone into the shroud, down by Larson's feet, then bound it there with strips of sail. For a seaman he did a slovenly job, but Crowe was a lazy man with rope and lashings, and every line he touched was left in a terrible tangle. When he finished, the shroud looked like the work of a spider, with its tattered threads flying in tresses. "Tak' the head," he told me, and we heaved the body up to the bulwark and held it there as the *Dragon* gently rolled.

"We commit this body to the deep," said Captain Crowe. "May he rest in peace." Then he gave a shove, and Larson tumbled from the rail, down toward the sea. The stone hit the hull with a thump, and I heard the *shush* of the cloth as it scraped along the planking. The bundle hit the water, and spray came up, icy cold.

We stared down from the rail, side by side. Captain Crowe, his hands braced, leaned far from the ship to stare aft down the hull. "It's no a bad way to go," said he. "I'd rather that than—" He stopped, and he leaned farther from the rail, until I thought he might topple right over the side. "By the saints," he whispered.

Against the planks, by the mainmast shrouds, Larson floated to the surface. Scraps of cloth billowed in twisted strands from his fingers and his arms, as though he had frantically torn himself loose from the shroud. The band I'd tied around his chin was the only thing still in place, and it gave his face an awful, tight-lipped smile.

He went bumping down the side and in below the counter, tapping at the hull as the *Dragon* surged on past him.

With Captain Crowe behind me, I ran toward the stern, past Dasher at the wheel, who shouted out, "What's the matter? What's gone wrong?"

Larson floated in the *Dragon*'s wake, tossing about in the foam from the counter. We saw his head and then his heels, his arms and legs together. We saw his hands reach up and flounder at the surface, and we saw his face as he somersaulted after us, the eyes wide open in a look that seemed like horror.

Even Dasher came to watch, and without him at the wheel, the *Dragon* wavered along on her course, and the wake stretched back in lazy curves. But no matter how the ship turned, Larson followed close behind, trapped in the swirl of water like a stick at the base of a falls.

"I don't like this," said Dasher. "I don't care for this at all."

"More canvas!" cried the captain. "Set the staysail. Main topsail too." He whirled round and looked forward up the deck. The wheel turned left and right, snubbing up against the loop of line that Dasher had thrown across the king spoke. "We'll see how fast a dead man swims."

Again I took the wheel. Dasher shouted for the others, and they tumbled together from the fo'c's'le. They seemed a furtive, scuttling pair, content to lie in darkness until they were called, the way the ghost of Drake was said to wait for the beating of a drum. One of them had come to me in the shadows, but I had no idea which it was, and neither gave a sign.

The wind rose from astern. It caught the sails and cracked them open, and I felt the *Dragon* rushing forward. Her deck aslant, her rigging taut and humming, she raced for France with a roar of water.

And the dead man came behind her.

Chapter 8
DASHING
TOMMY DUSKER

*I*n half a gale of wind, the *Dragon* left the land astern. She plunged along with too much sail but couldn't outrun the corpse. Trapped by the flow of water, spun by whirls and eddies, it followed in the churning foam. And the gulls came down in crowds.

I could hear them as I steered the schooner south, and I saw their shadows fly across the deck and the mass of sails. But not once did I look back; the clamor of their voices as they pecked upon the corpse was bad enough.

"I'll tak' the wheel," said Captain Crowe when the sails were set and drawing. I gave up my place, and we stood together on a slanted deck as the ship leaned far to starboard. The gulls clustered all round us, and the captain flinched whenever one came close.

"Gives me the frights," said he. "A dead man off the stern."

In his hands, the spokes looked thin as pencils. He

wrenched them hard and sent the *Dragon* on a weaving course. Then he took a glance behind him, but only that.

Dasher, in his bulging vest of corks, stood right at the stern with a boat hook in his hands. He jabbed it down toward the water, then flailed it through the air, beating at the seagulls that circled round him.

"It's worse for him," said Captain Crowe. "It haunts him, things like this. Poor Dasher gets the willies in an awful way, an' he's got no heart for seeing things harmed."

"Do you know him well?" I asked with more than idle curiosity.

Crowe stiffened at the wheel. It was just a tiny gesture, in his shoulders and his hands. "Whit are ye driving at?" he asked, and I heard impatience in his voice.

"The highwayman," I said. "The man who shot my father. He was a little bit like Dasher."

"Like Dasher?" said Crowe. He laughed. "There's no one like Dasher but Dasher hisself."

I told him all about that night on the lonely road. How *someone* had shot at my father, and how Larson had chased him off.

"He talked the way Dasher talks," I said. "He moved the same and laughed the same."

"Och, I canna see it," said Captain Crowe. "Dasher alone in the forest? In the darkness, no less? I don't think so, lad. Years I've known Dasher, and, och, he hasna got it in him."

"But the way he talks . . ."

"Och, he's *a'* talk," said Crowe. "Talk an' bluster, no more than that. He lives in a wee cottage wi' his wife and seven bairns. Every one an angel."

He was telling the truth, I could see, as far as he knew it. If Dasher really was the highwayman, there would be no one more surprised than Turner Crowe.

"Ye see those corks he wears?" asked he. "When Dasher was just a lad, he all but drowned. He slipped under a box that he carried, and it pinned him like a beetle to the mud. When they fished him out, he was near as dead as that corpse back there, and afeared o' the sea ever since." He motioned with his thumb. "That's oor Dasher: scared o' the water, scared by the wind, and fit to be tied at the sight o' his shadow."

"Then why's he a sailor?" I asked.

"Dasher?" The captain laughed. "Dasher's no sailor."

So he wasn't a highwayman, and he wasn't a sailor. "Then what is he?" I asked.

"Why, he's Dasher," said Captain Crowe. Apparently he thought this explained it all. He wrenched the wheel again, and the *Dragon* turned so sharply that the mainsail boom buried its tip in the sea.

On the stern, Dasher soared above me as the schooner heeled and dipped her bow. His legs apart, his hair in tangles, he slashed at the gulls with his boat hook. For a moment he looked like a knight, a fantastic knight who jousted with clouds and birds. Then the *Dragon* turned the other way and Dasher dropped below me until there was only the sea behind him, speckled with whitecaps. And out of the froth of the wake came Larson's hands as he cartwheeled along behind us.

"Is he still there?" asked Captain Crowe.

"Yes," I said.

"Seven knots," he said, and turned his hands around the spokes. "She's making seven knots or more." To the stern he looked, and then to the bow again. "Mathew thinks it's you," he said. "And what Mathew thinks, so thinks Harry. They say ye're a troll. Ye're bewitched."

"Your lashings came loose," I told him pointedly. "That's the only reason he's floating back there."

"Ye're mad," said Crowe. "It's a sign, ye see. He's waiting for another."

"Who?"

"The dead man!" shouted Captain Crowe. "He follows the ship because another will join him."

It was the first I had heard of that sailors' tale, and it gave me a shiver of fear. There were only five of us aboard the *Dragon.*

"Off wi' ye," said Crowe. "Let me be alone."

I went right to the eyes of the ship, then out to the bowsprit, and I sat astride to ride it, in the finest spot there was to watch the seas go by. I leaned forward until my chest touched the spar; I wrapped my arms around it and stared at the water foaming through the dragon's mouth.

The wooden jaws rose and fell. They seemed to bite at the waves, to chew them into froth. The head vanished altogether, then leapt from the sea, straining water through the teeth. The yellow eyes shone fierce with spray as the enormous head reared up, then plunged again. And in the sounds of the water, the dragon seemed to roar and breathe.

I watched the sun go down from there. I saw the sky turn pink and red, and I was filled with an awful doubt. *"You will come directly to London,"* my father had written, but I was rushing off in the other direction. If I went to Crowe and said, "Turn the ship around," what would he do? Was he the one the sailor had warned me about, or was it Dasher? *"The one least likely,"* the man had said. But surely it couldn't be Mathew or Harry. What reason would they have to harm me? And in that very thought, I realized it could be anyone at all.

At nightfall we left the corpse behind. It fell away slowly, farther and farther astern, and the gulls went with it, until they were all we could see—a ball of wheeling birds flashing in the twilight.

Captain Crowe called me aft and gave me the wheel. The wind rose, and rose again, until every sheet and halyard, every brace and guy, was strained as tight as an iron rod. The clouds came streaming in behind us, and there was no moon that night, no glow of stars. I stood my trick at the wheel in the faint light of the binnacle box, on a deck that heaved and quivered. The waves seemed to wait, then leap up at us as we came, shattering on the bow with a shock that I felt through the rudder and the spokes in my hands. It was all I could do to keep the *Dragon* anywhere near her course.

But we never touched the sails; we never did a thing to ease her passage, though the wind was ever rising. And when the helm became too much for me, Dasher lent a hand. On the leeward side, he had to press the spokes as I pulled them up, and we worked the wheel like a seesaw.

"What a night," said he. "What a blooming night. I must have rats in me attic to be out in a wind like this."

"Why *are* you here?" I asked.

"Why's anyone anywhere? That's the question." He was taller than me by head and shoulders, but the slant of the deck put our faces almost level. "It's money, my friend. Silver and gold."

"I want to hear silver jingle," the highwayman had said. *"Silver and gold."*

"It's why you're here yourself," said Dasher. "It's why the dead man's where he is and why I'm here beside you. The world's a bit of clockwork, and money is the pendulum, the weight that keeps it ticking. Why, it was money shot your father."

"What?" I said. "How do you know that?"

Dasher shrugged. "That's what I hear. That's what the Haggis told me."

"He *did?*" I asked, surprised and not a little angry. So Captain Crowe had gone straight to Dasher with my story.

"Now, don't get angry," Dasher said. "He asked me was I there, that was all."

His whiskers shivered in the wind, and his grin was bright as lanterns. Whenever he moved, the corks on his jerkin squeaked like old hinges.

"I told him that I might have been. I'm not saying I was, but I might have been. Oh, I'm a terror, John. From Romney Marsh to Ramsgate they know the name of Dashing Tommy Dusker."

He spoke the words in a fiery way, then shook his head to set his hair a-flying. In the glow of the binnacle light, his eyes sparkled like lavender jewels.

"You might have heard of me in London," he said.

"No," I said. "I haven't."

His grin faded into a look of sadness. "Well, you will," he said. "There'll come a day you'll hear of me. They might have to hang me first, but hear of me you will. They'll speak my name in every corner of the empire. In the colonies and Trinidad they'll say, 'Sure I know of Tommy Dusker.' And in the next breath, 'But who's the king, you say?' "

He raised his head then and watched the mainsail luff. His eyes seemed far away. And I could see in that look that Dasher was a harmless soul, full of talk and fancies.

He pressed on the wheel as the *Dragon* thundered through a wave. "He's all right now, isn't he?" Dasher asked.

"Who?" I said.

"Your father."

"Yes," I said. "He's fine."

Still Dasher didn't look toward me. He nodded. "That's good, then."

The wind blew hard but steady, and on we ran across the Channel. The glint that came from the binnacle box was the only light in all the world, as though the *Dragon* were a magical thing that carried the sun from dark to dawn. From a distance, I thought, the schooner would look like a spark racing through the night. But somewhere around us, I remembered, another ship was plunging along on the same course, heading for the same little port and the same cargo of contraband.

What if she got there before us? I wondered. We might go sailing in and find that our cargo had vanished. What would Captain Crowe say if I'd brought him all this way for nothing?

And then a worse thought occurred to me. What if the smugglers *didn't* get there before us? What if they arrived to find us there already?

Chapter 9
THE HOME OF NIGHTMARES

That year was one of peace between England and France, but for most of my life the countries had been at war, and I had grown up to fear the French as bogeymen and savages. In the shadows below my childhood bed, in the frosted patterns of the windows, it hadn't been beasts that lurked, nor ghosts, nor spirits, but cruel and sneering Frenchmen.

And so it was with trepidation that I watched the shore loom closer and saw it turn from black to gray as the night became the dawn. A streak of white etched across the darkness became a line of surf, and behind it were only shadows. This was France, the home of all my nightmares, and it stretched ahead and off to port, a low and rolling land that looked very much like Kent.

The wind that had driven us straight from the Downs began to ease at daybreak, as though its task were done. No longer was the *Dragon* pressed to her rails in the sea, flinging herself from wave to wave. She moved along like a stately thing, and I stood my last watch alone at the wheel until Captain Crowe sent me away.

He brought the signal flags, a bright little bundle of blue and white and yellow. "Hoist these," he said. "Then off with ye, lad. I know these waters well, and I'll tak' her in myself."

It was the oddest pair of flags that a ship had ever flown, one a sign of entering a port, and one a sign of leaving. Captain Crowe watched as I pulled them up the halyard and then remarked, with a dry wit, "They won't know if we're coming or going."

The blue peter above, the yellow jack below, they fluttered in the failing wind. I thought again of Father and hoped he would approve of what I'd done. The *Dragon*, for all intents, was now a smuggler, and I alone had set her to that business. France lay right before us, and the *Dragon* plowed toward it.

I went back to my place at the eyes of the ship, feeling in some foolish way that the farther forward I was, the sooner I would get there. Below me, the carved dragon took the seas in its teeth and gnashed them into foam. And I watched the land go by, a league to port—little squares of houses, the different greens of field and forest. All the sea was ours, and whatever strange ship it was that shared our voyage, she was nowhere to be seen.

The land came slowly closer, as though it spread itself toward us. Then we passed a rocky cape, and it seemed to open like a door, to show a village in a bay behind it, a harbor for the *Dragon*.

Dasher went shouting through the ship, and up came Mathew and Harry. We struck the topsails and then the foresail as we came behind the headland. There, in the shelter of the cape, the sea went suddenly smooth, the wind turned light and fitful. And under main and jib we went in spurts and dashes, through a flock of fishing boats that floated on their moorings, past a little brig and a tiny English ketch.

I heard a squeak, and Dasher came beside me, bulging with his corks. "That's the *Dover Girl*," said he, pointing to the ketch. "A fine old smuggler. Here for tea, no doubt. Tea and pilchards."

She floated so low in the water that her scuppers were nearly awash. Then we passed to leeward of her, through a stench of rotten fish. It was so thick that I could almost *see* the odor wafting from her hatches.

"She'd best be on her way," I said.

Dasher laughed. "Oh, she'll wait another day at least. It might be a hot one."

"But the fish," I said. "They won't be worth a ha'penny then."

"Of course they won't," said Dasher. "But they'll cover the smell of the tea. If you were a revenue man, would you shovel your way through that?"

I had never heard of this trick of the smugglers. "How do you know that?" I asked.

"You live in Kent, you hear the talk," he said. Then, again, his rakish grin appeared. "And of course I've done it, eh? What about that? Oh, I've led the king's cutters on many a fine chase. Had them running in circles out in the

Channel, like a lot of dogs with their tongues hanging out. The revenue? Oh, they live in dread of Dashing Tommy Dusker."

"I'm sure they do," said I, just as sure they didn't.

He strutted like a peacock. "You're a lucky lad to be sailing with me. The stories you'll have for your father!" He slapped me on the shoulder, then pointed across the bay. "Now, that other one," he said. "That brig there."

"She looks too small to carry anything," I said.

"False bottoms," said he, with a wink. "They'll load her when the tide is out. Stuff her full of barrels that you'd have to be a fish to see."

"And then beach her on the other side to get them out again."

"Why, yes," he said. "Oh, you're quick, you are. Born to this, I think."

I should have been angry, but Dasher's comment—oddly—left me feeling proud. Certainly Father gave me small praise, and I suppose it was merely pleasant to hear Dasher's words, no matter how ill meant they were. I leaned against the rail, feeling inflated and light, as we sailed across the harbor.

On the southern shore, the buildings rose above a quay. They were tall and thin—so narrow that the row of them might have been squashed together in a giant's vise. Built from brick of different colors, from wood and stone, they seemed to tilt and lean, like tramps in tattered clothes once too often patched.

Crowe steered us toward a wharf crowded with piles of barrels, with stacks of bales and boxes. Cranes and hoists stood among them, their slender arms held high and crossed in every way. Wagons came and went, drawn by plodding horses. And in the bustle, like a rock that the tide flows around, was a small old man, frail and dressed in rags. From his nose and ears grew clumps of white hair. He watched us from the barrels, on a perch among the stacks, now leaning forward and now back, now holding his hands to his head like blinkers.

We glided toward the quay. The old man stood up on the barrels. "Turner Crowe!" he shouted, and his voice was strange and otherworldly. It was a haunting voice. "Turner Crowe," he said again. "Do you remember me, you butcher?"

Crowe's head snapped round. "By the saints!" he breathed.

"You didn't kill us all," the old man wailed. "There's one alive. There's one to tell the tale." Then down he got and scuttled off, moving like an old white beetle in among the wagons and the bundles.

"Wait!" shouted Crowe. His face was bloodless. "Heave to, ye old bodach!" His hands shook at the spokes so hard, the rudder rattled.

I looked at Dasher. "Who was that?"

"Don't know," said he. And then, suddenly, "I have to get forward. Stand by to lower the jib; strike the halyard; get a lashing on." And off he went, with a flick of his hair, leaving me alone at the rail.

The quay was slung with enormous fenders of woven rope. But Captain Crowe brought the *Dragon* alongside so perfectly that they made no sound at all. If they'd been eggs, he wouldn't even have cracked them.

Crowe called me to the wheel, then took my arm in his fist. "Ye're to watch for that white-haired man. Watch for him, hear? And if ye see him, ye fetch me."

"Who is he?" I asked.

His hand tightened fiercely. "Do ye have to question everything I say? I've telt ye to watch for him, and that's a' ye need to know."

"Yes, sir," I said. I was used to his anger; again I saw it engulf him completely, then vanish in a moment.

"Good lad," he said, and smiled. "Ye're a credit to the ship, and I'll be telling your father as much."

Already the *Dragon* was tied to the wharf, her bowsprit overhanging the quay. Mathew and Harry broke open the hatches and dropped down to the hold. Then the cargo came across, barrel after barrel. Two and three at once, hung in slings of net, they were swung across and lowered through the hatches. The Frenchmen worked with a fever that I'd never seen at any dock in London.

Captain Crowe watched it from the rail, his head swinging back and forth to follow the path of the barrels. When a sling came loose and the nest of barrels lurched, then caught, he bellowed at the men who worked the hoist. He spoke, much to my surprise, in French, though his accent was abysmal.

"*Prenez garde* there!" he shouted. "*En douce*, ye Froggy bastards." And he stomped up and down the deck, muttering as he tugged at the white cravat around his neck.

I was deeply troubled to see him at a business he clearly knew well. I had imagined we would load our cargo amid suspicion and secrecy, without a word being said. But Captain Crowe was no stranger to these Frenchmen.

They delighted in his bluster and collapsed in laughter when he spoke. One, a small man in enormous boots, his face nothing more than a flowing mustache, walked behind him, mocking his seaman's roll. And the others, laughing, accidentally let a barrel tumble from its sling to shatter on the bulwark. The overpowering smell of brandy covered the ship in an instant. And in the next, a score of Frenchmen threw themselves to the deck, dabbing with their fingers at a pool of spirits so potent that it had no color at all.

"I'm no paying for that!" bellowed Captain Crowe. "*Levez-vous!* Back to work, ye mangy dogs. And don't forget the barley sugar; I've got to color every drap o' that."

I felt a shiver of despair. I wished I had never come to France.

He saw me watching, and turned his anger onto me. "Whit are ye gawking at?" he said. "Ye were telt to stand a watch."

"You're *paying* for this?" I asked.

"Ye think they give it away?" He spread a hand across his face and squeezed with thumb and fingers. And slowly the color drained from his skin. He dragged his hand across his nose, across his mouth and chin. He *scraped* away his anger.

"Look," he said. "Use some sense, lad. Ye canna just come waltzing in and waltzing out wi' cargo." He took my arm and bent closer; his cravat tickled my chin as he whispered in my ear. "If they think for a moment that a' that brandy's no waiting for the *Dragon,* then the game's up right there and then."

I shook off his arm. "They know you here," I said. "You speak French; you knew which dock to come to."

"Whit are ye saying?"

"Don't cross him," Dasher had said. But it was too late for that. I squared myself up beside him. "I think you're a smuggler, Captain Crowe."

His mouth fell open; he gaped at me. I waited for a rage like none he'd shown before, and cringed when he raised his arm. But he didn't strike me. He only scratched his ear, and he hung his head like a repentant child. "It's true enough," said he. "I *was* a smuggler. To my everlasting shame, I was." He turned his back to me. "But no more, Mr. Spencer. That Burton gang the manny wrote about? I want to see it ruined. I want to see every one o' they villains hanging from a gallows."

"Hanging?" I said. "That's not the way you talked at the Baskerville."

"Och, that's a' it was, is talk." He sat on the rail, and his toe scraped at the deck. "I remember when I first saw ye, your father and yourself," he said. "At the old Baskerville, mind. I thought your father was the doubter, the one to smell the smoke where there wasna any." He glanced up, then down again. "Yet now he trusts me wi' his ship and his very own son, but yourself, ye give me none at a'."

He seemed truthful enough, but I'd seen his acts before.

"Ye're a careful one," said Crowe. "That's good; I like that in a man." He fumbled at the cloth below his chin.

"Weel, look at this," he said as he whisked away the white cravat. It was the first time I'd seen his neck, and around it was a livid welt of frightening proportions.

"They tried to hang me," said Captain Crowe. "The smugglers did. It's whit they do to they who turn against them."

I could see the patterns of the rope burned upon his skin, the weaving of its strands in bright and shocking red. I could imagine how tight the noose had drawn, how he must have gasped for breath.

"I've a score to settle," said he, already covering the mark again. "And that's why I'm here, do ye see?"

"And the white-haired man?"

"He was one o' them," said Crowe. "He'd like nothing better than to slit my throat for what I did to wreck that gang. So tak' my glass, lad—it's by the binnacle—and get yourself up to the crosstrees. Watch for him there. And mind, too, that ye watch for a sail in the offing. If that smuggler comes, she'll likely be armed to the teeth."

I still didn't trust the man, not fully. But there was no undoing what I had done by bringing us here. So I climbed up to the crosstrees and sat with my back against the mast. Through the captain's long glass, I studied the Channel and the land around us, as the sounds of the loading—a rumble of barrels—went on below me. Once I thought I saw the white-haired man flitting over the crowded quay. Round a team of horses, past a derrick, past a wagon, he was just a movement at the corner of my eye. Then he vanished in the curve below the *Dragon*'s bow, and I trained my spyglass there. But he never came out on the other side, and he never went back again. If I had seen him at all, he had disappeared.

The sun crossed above the mast and started down before our job was finished. But at last I heard the thump of hatches slamming closed and looked down to see the men tramping from the deck. Our signal flags were lowered and our lines were cast away. And the *Dragon*, freed again, headed for the sea.

Where once we had run before the wind, now we tacked against it. Back and forth across the harbor, shore to shore, we went. At each side we rounded up and turned again. Stuffed with barrels, the *Dragon* was slow and almost sluggish. But the tide was behind her, and she beat her way from the sheltered harbor and out beyond the cape.

No longer did she rise to meet the waves. She battered through them, drenched with spray; she lunged, and tossed, and smashed a passage north toward the shores of England.

And before another dawn had risen, one of us aboard her would die upon her decks.

Chapter 10
CANNONS IN THE FOG

F rance was wreathed in fog, twenty miles behind us, when a sail was sighted far to windward. Captain Crowe took his spyglass and climbed the mainsail hoops, "to have a squint," said he.

Mathew and the cook were huddled at the bows. Dasher was beside me at the wheel. I kept the *Dragon* by the wind and held her steady on her course. But still the captain swung madly across the sky, clinging to the wooden bands as the schooner thrashed along. Though the wind was warm, the spray was bitterly cold, and he wore his boat cloak now to shield himself against it. The cloth flapped against his arms and streamed out behind him.

From the deck, the distant sail looked like nothing more than another whitecap among the thousands leaping in the Channel. Yet even as I watched, it grew larger, looming up from the seas, as though a swirl of spindrift had taken shape to come bearing down upon us.

"A cutter," shouted Captain Crowe. "Coming fast. She's laid a course across our bows."

Already I could see the curves of her headsails. She was flying toward us, down the wind.

"Come about!" roared Captain Crowe.

I spun the wheel. The *Dragon* hurled herself across the waves, and the men at the bows leapt toward the jib sheets. Captain Crowe, halfway to the crosstrees, was tossed from side to side as the mast came straight and heeled again. His cloak billowed up around his head, and he beat it down as he struggled with the spyglass.

The approaching sail grew wider.

"She'll come behind us now," shouted Captain Crowe. He swung the spyglass from bow to stern and round again, as though he might find a place in that empty sea in which to hide a schooner.

The cutter was faster than our *Dragon,* and she slowly grew as she closed the distance. She was thirty tons or more.

Captain Crowe came down the hoops. He went straight to the weather rail. In his hands, the spyglass shrank and grew, and it made a tapping sound as the pieces slid together. "Twenty miles to France," he said. "Twenty miles to home. Whatever we do, they devils there will run us doon like dogs."

"Who are they?" I asked.

He gave me barely a glance. "Who do ye think?" said he.

The smugglers, of course. They had waited out the weather and found us now fleeing for home, laden with the cargo that was theirs. *"She'll likely be armed to the teeth,"* the captain had said. And he watched her now with fear in his eyes.

"She's got the weather gauge," he said. "Damn this wind." He peered over the side, then off toward the cutter. "Bring her a point to leeward," he shouted at me. "By and large, ye hear?"

Dasher grinned. "By and large. Oh, there's a lovely bit of talk."

I spun the wheel, and the *Dragon* lurched around to take the waves farther down her side. The sails bellied full, and she hurried along, faster now by a knot or more. "By and large," I said.

The *Dragon* thundered on across the Channel, and all of us aboard watched by turns the sea ahead and the cutter behind. I could see the power in her swollen, bulging sails, and her bowsprit, now thrusting from the sea.

"Three hours and she'll be on us," said Captain Crowe.

Our bowsprit climbed above the waves, then dropped and rose again in a plume of silvered mist. I heard the roaring from the dragon figurehead and the thrumming of the mainsail leech, loud and steady.

The waves came tumbling down and pitched us over, and the mainsail boom slammed against the sea. The sails were spattered dark with spray, pouring water from tack and clew, as though the *Dragon* sweated from her headlong rush to England.

I could feel the weight she carried. It dragged her down and made the sea run high and thick around her counter. No longer did she gallop like a magical stallion; she'd become a draft horse, fat and trudging, maned with spindrift.

And the cutter closed the distance.

"She goes better with a corpse behind her," said Dasher, with a nervous laugh. "Where's a dead man when we need one?"

"Stow it," said Crowe. He stood at the weather rail, his fingers hooked like talons to the wood, his cloak tangled in the wind. He looked like a part of the ship, not moving at all as the deck rolled and plunged. He never took his eyes from the cutter.

The other two had moved to the foremast shrouds, as close to the stern as ever I'd seen them, except for their turns at the wheel. They held to the ropes and peered to windward, and again I wondered which of them had come to me in the darkness. And was the other the man I had to fear, *the one least likely*? I studied their faces, but neither gave the slightest sign of seeing me there at all. As one man, they watched the cutter. All of us, we watched it coming closer.

Then, suddenly, Dasher started singing. His voice was rich and powerful, his song so deeply sad that I felt it beating time within my heart. On the vastness of the stormy sea, in the peril of that moment, I felt as though he sang us to our doom. The cutter came in full sight, the water splitting across her bow into tumbling streaks of foam. She heeled and straightened, dipped toward us and away, and I saw the men, thirty or more, upon her decks.

Dasher sang; he faced ahead, and the spray ran like tears along his whiskers.

"He rode the highways of the night;
His milestones were the stars.
Past Polaris and Andromeda,
Round Jupiter and Mars."

At the cutter's bow, a tarpaulin mushroomed in the wind. It flew away to leeward, and a dozen men fought to bring it in. And underneath it, gleaming black, was the barrel of a cannon.

There was a cry from forward, and Mathew thrust an arm through the shrouds, pointing at the cutter. Captain Crowe seemed to tilt toward the sea as the *Dragon* rolled to windward. And Dasher sang with aching melancholy.

"A phantom horse of moonstone shod
A rider swathed in shrouds
And a maiden fair who longs to hear
His thunder in the clouds."

"Shut up, I told you!" roared Captain Crowe. He whirled round, his face red with anger. "Batten down your trap, ye hear?"

The song dwindled into nothing, and I heard again the roaring of the sea, the drumbeat of the mainsail.

"Ye great dandified noddy. Ye lummox," bellowed Captain Crowe. He was either very angry or very, very scared. "I'm sick o' ye. I'm sick o' your larks and your airs. And I'm sick o' the sight o' they damned corks ye're aye wearing."

The grin trembled on Dasher's lips. He tried to hold it there but couldn't, and he turned away, as though to study the sea at the leeward rail. The *Dragon* rolled, and the tilt of the deck made me soar above him, until he seemed very small, like a little boy dressed for a childish game in his pathetic suit of corks.

"Ye're a blether," said the captain, still ranting at Dasher. "Ye're full o' prattle and rubbish. No heart for killing, ye say. Weel, I hope to hear ye singing when ye're dancing in a noose." Then he turned on me, his eyes like furnace doors. "And you," he said. "I should—"

His sentence went unfinished. A cloud of smoke jetted from the cannon's mouth, and a long moment later the sound reached us. It shook the very air; it rattled in my bones. Then the sea beyond our bowsprit erupted in a geyser, and already the tiny, distant figures were swabbing out the barrel.

"They missed," I said.

"Och, they weren't aiming for us, ye gowk!" yelled the captain.

Dasher smiled at me. A pathetic smile. "Not yet," he said. "But soon enough, my friend. A warning shot, was all that was. And when they tire of their little game, they'll bring the sticks down, John. Just you wait and see."

Captain Crowe pushed me from the wheel. He took the spokes in his enormous fists and sent the *Dragon* reeling down the wind. So suddenly did he turn the ship that I barely kept my balance. Dasher didn't; he fell across the planks with a thud and squeal, as though his corks were mice that he had landed on.

We twisted through the waves, and the cutter twisted with us, coming always closer. Again we saw the cannon fire; again we heard the awful thunder of its blast, then saw the ball land close ahead. With every puff of smoke I cringed inside, for a ball of iron weighing nine pounds or more was rushing through the air, and it seemed the gun was aimed at only me.

Captain Crowe turned his face toward the wind and sniffed. "Ye smell that?" he asked.

I shook my head.

"Fog. I dinna see it, but I smell it right enough." He went up on his toes, squinting like a badger. "A few minutes more; that's all we need."

"Show them a flag," said I. "The ensign."

He frowned. "Och, ye're daft."

"No," I said. "We could hoist it, and . . . They wouldn't shoot at the ensign, would they?"

Crowe stared at me. Then his face twisted into his old and cunning smile. "O' course," he said. "Damn my eyes, I might have thought o' that myself." He laughed and clapped my shoulder. "Ye've got the wheel," he said, and took himself below.

Dasher had hauled himself up from the deck. He adjusted his corks and shook his hair. "He's a mean old cove," he said. "But he's never wrong about the fog."

In a moment Crowe was back, and he thrust a bundled flag into my hands. "Here," he said. "Dasher, give him a hand."

We clapped the ensign on the halyard, and the wind tore it loose into a flurry of white and red and blue. But in our haste, I saw, we'd set it upside down, the sign of a ship in trouble.

"Leave it," said Dasher. "We're in distress all right, I guess." But I turned it straight, and hand over hand we hoisted the flag to the gaff. It snapped and flogged against the topping lift, the big red cross and the Union Jack flashing in the wind.

Dasher gazed up at it, then aft at the cutter. "Oh, they're talking now," he said. "They're wondering, all right. 'That's a king's ship up there,' they're saying. And now there's someone asking, 'Why's the navy running like a thief?' " He laughed. "That's a sight they won't see every day."

The flag gained us only a moment. Then the cutter, rolling on a crest, fired again, far across our bow. And a dab of color appeared at her peak, streaming in the wind. They had hoisted the same white ensign.

"Oh, that's droll," said Dasher. "Sometimes I think we're *all* in the navy out here."

I watched the distant flag curl and stiffen from the cutter's gaff. It was a strange sort of joke, I thought, for a smuggler to answer our ensign with another. I said, "Maybe it *is* the navy. That might be a revenue cutter."

"Too far to tell," said Dasher.

"I'll fetch the captain's spyglass."

I turned to go, but Dasher held me back. "Too late for that," he said.

For a moment I was angry, and I tried to shake off his hand. But Dasher had caught me off balance, and I stumbled back against the cushion of his corks. One of them broke loose and bounced across the deck.

"Look there," he said, pointing at the cutter.

A band of clouds, laced with blue and yellow, tumbled in

behind her, rising up in feathered wisps like steam upon a cauldron. The sky grew darker; the sea began to simmer.

"Fog," cried Dasher. He laughed; he danced a little jig. "Bless that poor old Captain Haggis. He's right again. He always is."

It came quickly then, spreading across the water, billowing up against the sun. It touched the cutter and made a ghost of her, a gray and frightful ghost.

And the pattern of her shooting changed. With a shriek that scared the daylights from me, a ball passed overhead. It left a round and perfect hole in the belly of the mainsail, like a piece of sky pasted on the canvas. And the next shot came right after, in a moment that was utter terror. I heard the whistle of the ball and, already looking up, saw the tip of the foresail gaff shatter into splinters.

Dasher ducked behind the rail. His face looked suddenly old, suddenly very scared. "Oh, ho!" said he, with a grimace meant to be a grin. "They're down to business now."

And the cutter vanished altogether.

A waft of fog seemed to hang above the *Dragon*'s bow, then swirl around the masts. We raced through it, and through another after, and then the sun went out, and all our world was white. I couldn't see as far as the wheel; I could hardly see the water right below. And with every nerve atingle, I waited for the next ball to come speeding straight toward me.

The *Dragon* tilted heavily as Captain Crowe brought her up to windward. But he wasn't quick enough. I heard again that dreadful whistle, and right behind it a human scream, an awful, chilling shriek. The *Dragon*, head to wind, shivered like a frightened horse, and the scream rose high, then went on and on.

"He's done for," Dasher said, cowering by the rail. In his voice I heard the horror that I felt. "Good God, the captain's dead."

Chapter 11
NO TASTE FOR BLOOD

We ran forward through the fog and found the wheel empty, turning by itself. Of Captain Crowe there was no sign at all, as though he'd vanished from the schooner. Dasher was almost frantic. He looked down in the scuppers and behind the binnacle.

"Captain Crowe!" he shouted. "Captain Crowe!"

The familiar old voice came back, with neither distance nor direction. "Stop your hooting, will ye? I'm here."

"Where?" asked Dasher. And stupidly he looked toward the rigging.

"Here, ye daft gowk," bellowed Captain Crowe. "By the foremast."

"Go," said I, and took the wheel. I turned it hard to leeward, and the *Dragon*—half aback—fell slowly off the wind. But Dasher worked himself in front of me.

"I'll steer," he said. "Please. I've got no taste for blood."

I only stared at him. This was Dashing Tommy Dusker, too frightened to go forward and tend to an injured man?

"Please," he said again. "It makes me queasy. Just the thought of blood does me rather poorly."

I left him there and went forward myself. By the time I reached the mainmast, the schooner had gathered way. When I reached the foremast she was sailing again, prancing along.

Down on the deck, his back to me, sat Captain Crowe. In his arms he held a body. A hand, red with blood, clawed at his shoulder. The head slumped back on one side; the legs jutted out on the other, toes turned inward.

"What happened?" I asked.

Captain Crowe tipped his head. "Stay there!" he barked. "Ye dinna have to see this."

"Is he dead?" I asked.

"He's wishing that he was."

I was aware then of the other man watching. Harry, the cook, stood by the mast in the edge of the fog, as silent as a figure carved from stone. He looked directly at me, eye to eye, but whether with fear or hate or tenderness I could not tell at all.

"Go on," said Captain Crowe. "Awa' wi' ye now."

The hand of the dying sailor clamped tighter onto the captain's shoulder. His head writhed side to side, but the feet moved not at all. From end to end he looked to be seven feet in length. But Mathew was not nearly as tall as that.

I was sure, in that moment, that he was the one who had warned me of danger. And I was sure that someone had killed him in the cover of the fog. I stepped closer and looked down, and—

The man was cut in two. The cannonball, or something, had torn right through him, and now his blood and innards were spilling out across the captain's lap. It was a sight that nearly drove me to my knees: poor Mathew's wretched look of horror, the gap between his torso and his legs. I reeled away, back toward the wheel, where Dasher caught me and sat me down.

"Was it bad?" said he. "I guess it was. Oh, Lord, I can see that it was."

Before long I heard a splash. And another after that. Then Captain Crowe came down the deck, past us to the stern. Wherever he walked, there were drops of red. He took off his cloak, bundled it up, and hurled it over the rail.

There were only four of us now on the *Dragon*, and we listened in dread to the sounds that came out of the fog. There was a creak of rope, a surge of water, and the terrible rumble of guns across a deck.

"So they've found us," said Crowe. He looked up, and I saw the streaks of blood, in four straight lines, that stretched across his cheek. "The fog's no high enough tae hide the masts," said he. "Dasher, get aloft. And you," he said to me, "ye've got the wheel."

Dasher went up the ratlines and disappeared, swallowed by the fog. I stared at a compass that seemed to swing wherever it wanted. In every direction was only whiteness; there was nothing to steer toward.

"Ye feel that?" said Captain Crowe. "The wind's going down."

It was. The water that had roared at the figurehead now passed with a muffled hush. The schooner stood more upright, and the sails had lost their fullness. It took a quarter turn of the great wooden wheel to do what a touch had done before.

"There she is!" cried Dasher suddenly. His voice came from above us.

"Where?" said Captain Crowe.

"Beside us there. Don't you see? Beside us, man."

I saw her then, the bowsprit first, next the jib and the enormous main. Like a shadow of the *Dragon* cast upon the fog, she slid along beside us.

"Bear away!" Captain Crowe commanded.

I turned the wheel, but not fast enough for him. He threw himself at it, and the king spoke cracked against my knuckles, then passed in a blur with the others. The *Dragon* whirled to leeward, and the cutter faded into nothing.

We turned to port, then hard to starboard. We ran with the jib aback, and we jibed across the wind, and the compass spun like a whirligig. The fog fiddled with my senses; I stared wildly at things that weren't there. Flotillas of fantastic ships, enormous faces, and even ladies walking on the water came and went on every side. But I could *hear* the cutter, the slap of water at her hull, the flapping of her sails.

"Where is she?" asked Captain Crowe. Then, loud enough that Dasher would hear, "Where the *devil* is she?"

Dasher shouted down, "On the port side now."

Crowe and I looked to the left, below the mainsail boom. I saw a shape loom up and disappear. A cannon fired wildly.

"Och, she's sailing circles round us," said Captain Crowe. He threw the helm down, and around we went again, like children at a deadly game of blindman's bluff, groping through the fog.

But the wind fell ever lighter. And the fog grew even thicker. "Like porridge," said Captain Crowe, a fair enough description. It was a bubbling gruel that filled the space between the masts and slowed the *Dragon* down.

Dasher came back to the deck. "Never seen a fog so thick," said he. "I'm going goggle-eyed from all the staring."

"If we canna see them, they canna see us," said Captain Crowe philosophically. But he had hardly spoken when another voice, a stranger's voice, came clearly through the fog.

"I hear them there," it said.

"Not a sound," said Crowe, his voice a rasping whisper. "Not a sound, ye hear?"

This voice without a shape was worse than the shadows in the fog. It raised an icy panic in the bottom of my spine. Then came the sounds of the ship, the wood and canvas and water. And another voice, a different one, hailed us from that void.

"Heave to," it said. "This is *Intrepid*. His Majesty's Ship *Intrepid*."

I laughed. I know how odd it sounds, but I laughed from sheer relief. These men weren't smugglers at all. "They're revenue," I said. "It's all right now; it's the revenue."

"Aye, so it is," said Captain Crowe.

I raised my hands to answer back, but the captain hauled them down. In a trice he had an arm around my throat, a

98

hand across my mouth. "There'll be no shouting," he said. "There'll be no sound at a'."

I fought against him, but he was far too strong. He ordered Dasher to the wheel, and he dragged me kicking toward the rail. He shoved me down and held me there, bent backward across the bulwark. Like a clamp across my jaw, his fingers pushed against me, until my feet lifted from the deck and I saw the water rushing past the hull.

His hand smelled of blood. He snarled like a vicious dog.

"If ye mak' a sound," he said, "so much as a squeak, I'll tip ye over the side."

Chapter 12
DEADLOCK

Somewhere in the fog, by the sounds I heard, the revenue cutter was coming about. Captain Crowe heard them, too, and he raised his great shaggy head to listen. In his hands I struggled like a dying fish, praying the ship would come across our bow. But the flap of sails and squeal of blocks grew only fainter, and at last disappeared. She had lost us in the fog.

Captain Crowe loosened his fingers, and it was all I could do to breathe again.

"Now," said he, "ye're a smart young lad. If ye give me your word that ye'll keep your mouth shut, we'll go on and finish the job."

I slumped down on the deck, my hands at my throat. In the mist at the mainmast, I saw Harry watching me.

"What will it be?" said Crowe. "The *Dragon*'s going to Dover. And when the brandy's off, ye can do as ye please.

So, tell me." He kicked my ribs. "Do ye give your oath? Ye'll never breathe a word o' this to any living soul?"

"I can't promise that," I said.

He shrugged. "Then I'll pitch ye over the side. It's a' the same to me."

He reached down, but I squirmed away. "You can't take the *Dragon*," I said. "What good's she to you?"

"No good at a'," said he, as calm as anything. "If I try to keep her, they'll hunt me like a pirate. But I can tak' her up to London, can't I, and tell that blasted father of yours how his poor, besotted son went ower the side in a storm. And he'll see me all weepin' and sad, and say, 'Why, bless your heart, Cap'n Crowe, here's a guinea for your troubles.'"

He stepped toward me; I scuttled backward.

"Och, laddie," he said. "Ye canna go far."

I knew he was right, and I had never felt so helpless. Wherever I ran, he could follow. He would toss me over the side without a thought, and I would drown in the *Dragon*'s wake, watching her shrink in the fog. I stood up and stepped back toward the mainmast.

"Take him, Harry," said Crowe.

I had no time to look behind me. I heard a footstep on the deck and felt arms encircling my chest. The cook held me in an iron grip, and his breath was hot and spongy on my neck.

"Just give me your word," said Crowe. "I ask no more than that."

"I won't," I said.

"Whit a shame," said Crowe. "Whit an affy shame." Then he grabbed me by the wrist and tore me away from Harry. He lifted me right from the deck and turned toward the rail. He held me there as the deck heaved up, and I knew I had but a moment left to live.

The *Dragon* shuddered at the peak of her roll. She started back, and the sea came soaring up toward us. And Crowe stepped closer to the side.

"Stop!" I cried. "I've got the book. I've got Larson's book!"

He hesitated. The deck dipped down toward the sea and slowly rose again. "Ye're grasping at straws," he said. But in his eyes I saw a doubt.

"You'll never find that book," I said. "But someone will. A week from now—a month from now—it will surely come to light. And they'll hang you then, and all your gang. They'll bind your arms and put a noose around your neck, and—"

"Shut up!" roared Captain Crowe.

My words had found their mark. He rubbed his big fists across his cheeks, smearing the dead man's blood. I felt as though I'd planted a bomb down in the depths of the ship and armed it with a slow match.

"It's all written in the book," I said. "The names of every smuggler." I spoke quickly, blurting it out. "Harry saw it. Ask him if he didn't."

Crowe stared at me with his glowering eyes. There was a glimmer there I'd never seen before—a hint of fear, I thought.

"Whit's he blethering about?" he asked.

"It's true," said Harry. "He's got the book; you gave it to him, Captain, sir. And full of names it is, Captain Crowe. I seen it for myself."

"Where is it, then?" asked Crowe. He cast me down to the scuppers, half against the rail. His enormous hand spread across my chest, and he held me to the deck. "Where is it?" he asked again.

"Somewhere safe," I told him. "I hid it down below."

"Ye hid it?" He barked a horrid laugh. "Weel, ye've got your wits about ye, I'll grant ye that. And now ye're going to go and fetch it." Then he added with a sneer, "If ye please, *Mister* Spencer."

"Why?" I asked. "So you can throw it with me over the side?"

I saw the veins pulsing in his neck, his teeth grinding hard together as a flash of anger burned through his fingers and into my arm. Then he shook himself, and his grip relaxed.

He said, "No one's going to hurt ye."

I feared him most of all in this mask of calm. "Listen, John," he said. "Give me the manny's book, and when we've got the barrels ashore, we'll go along to London. Your father gets his ship and cargo, he gets his profit—and a little more perhaps; aye, a little more—and that's the end o' the matter. No harm to no one."

With his narrow, folded eyes, his rows of teeth showing in a ghastly smile, he looked like a grinning snake. "No harm to no one," he said again.

"All right," I told him. It seemed I had no choice. "I'll give you the book."

"Fine." He let me go. He stared at me and frowned. "Well, fetch it, then."

"Not yet," said I. "When we get to London, when we're tied to Father's dock, *then* you get the book. But not before."

I heard Dasher laugh. "A deadlock," he said. "A lovely dilemma."

Captain Crowe drew out his knife and flicked it open. "Then I'll have to cut ye into pieces," he said calmly. "Your fingers and your toes, then your ears and eyes and lips. And what's left o' ye will tell me where it is, a' right."

"I won't," I said, though I feared the quaver in my voice gave away the lie.

"Oh, ye will," said he. Crowe took my hand and slapped it on the rail. He pressed the knife against the knuckle of my little finger. The blade rocked across my skin. "Tell me, son," he said. "Where is it?"

In the silver of his knife, I saw two hugely staring eyes, horror-struck: my own face reflecting back at me. I saw the blade cut through the skin and the blood ooze out with a shocking, awful redness. And worst of all was Captain Crowe, hunched above me, calmly slicing through my finger. *That* was the thing that brought a scream to my lips. Captain Crowe was smiling.

"You bloodthirsty pirate!" shouted Dasher. He came in a whirl across the deck and kicked the knife from the captain's hand. It flew off the rail and went spinning into the fog, glistening like a fallen star. "I'm not going to watch you cut up a boy. Not a lad and a shipmate. I'm not going to stand for that."

"Och, I'd never hae done it," said Captain Crowe. He had turned in an instant into a madman, in an instant back again. Now he stood and brushed his trouser knees. "You didna have to kick awa' my best knife, Dasher. That was my favorite knife."

"Just leave him to think," said Dasher. "He'll see the sense in the end." Then he went to the wheel and brought the *Dragon* back to her course. "Steady as she goes," he said. "By and large, that is."

Captain Crowe tugged at his jacket; he straightened his cravat. "Harry, come with me," he said, and the two went down below.

The *Dragon* sailed on, north toward England, through a fog that grew thick and then thin. I put my finger to my mouth and sucked away the blood, watching Dasher at the wheel, his jaunty self again. I hated to see him happy there, as though he had no other care at all, and hated even more to hear him start to sing.

"Stop that," I said.

He looked wounded.

"You're a dog in a doublet," I said.

He laughed. "What a thing to say! Didn't I save your bacon there? Didn't I risk my life and limb—"

"You knew it all along!" I cried. "As soon as you saw that cutter you knew she was a revenue ship. There *is* no other smuggler, and there never was. It's the *Dragon* that Larson wrote about. Right from the start it was the *Dragon* that was going to France."

"That's true enough," said Dasher. He grinned at the binnacle, then cocked up his chin and shook his hair. He had caught his own reflection in the compass glass.

"You must think me young and foolish," I said.

"Not at all," said Dasher, staring straight ahead. "You're too quick by half, and that's your trouble."

I didn't feel clever at all. The truth, I saw, had been right in front of me from the very first day. "Captain Crowe told me that Father had sent him new orders," I said. "But he can't read, can he? He told me that when I opened Larson's pouch."

"Are you still bleeding?" asked Dasher.

I looked at my finger. "No," said I.

Only then did he look toward me. "What's done is done," he said. "There's no comfort in a misery. But if you'd kept to yourself and asked no questions, we'd be running into Dover with the spirits, then on to London with the wool. You'd be going home the hero, and guineas richer for your troubles."

"Is that the way you planned it? You and Captain Crowe?"

"More me than him," said Dasher, beaming proudly. "He's a madman, Captain Haggis is. I'm the one what does the thinking for him. A fortnight to take the *Dragon* round to London? Why, that was plenty of time, I told him, to make a run to France and back. And then that Larson chap, that little gent, stumbled on it, didn't he? Lord knows how, but he did."

"And you killed him for it," I said.

"Not I!" Dasher shook his head. "There was no one more

surprised than I to see him swimming through the Downs, dead as a doornail. But he was mucking about in a smuggling gang, so it's no wonder he got himself killed. They all do, those who interfere."

"Like me?" I asked.

"Not if you watch your step," said Dasher. "Not if you give us the book."

It kept coming back to that waterlogged book and the pages of Larson's notes. *"The dead man's secrets,"* a sailor had called them. *"See you keep them safe."* I dreaded what might happen if I had no secrets left to keep.

"There's no hurry," said Dasher. "There's no rush. But you won't see London again until the Haggis has that book. And that's a fact, my friend."

He said all this with a cheerful smile that I found more unnerving than all the captain's rage. I picked myself up and wandered away, but Dasher called after me. "Where are you going?"

"Wherever I please," said I.

The fog was not as thick as it had been, and I knew he was watching as I went down the companionway. I heard a thumping up forward, and smiled to myself at the thought of the captain—or Harry, perhaps—searching for a book that wouldn't be found. Then I hurried through the schooner, back toward the stern. I opened the door of my little cabin . . . and found it all in ruin. The thin mattress had been pulled from my bunk, my sea bag torn open across it. My ledgers were strewn to the deck, kicked in a heap to the corner. Even my quill had been plucked from its pot and cast across the cabin.

Someone had gone through the room in a rage. But I found a small pleasure in the sadness of the place. No one would search there again.

My tinderbox lay behind the door. A candle — broken in the middle — was wedged behind the bunk. I shoved them in my pockets and went out to the narrow, tilting passageway.

To reach the lazarette, I had to pass the captain's cabin. The door was ajar, held by a hook and eye, and in the motion of the *Dragon* it rattled open and shut, with a sound like shaken bones. Through the gap I saw the captain, standing at a porthole. As I had seen him once before, he was talking to no one at all. Or talking to the ship. He touched the porthole gently, as he would a woman's face. So intent was he on this that I crept past without him seeing or hearing, and made my way to the lazarette.

The steering ropes were looser than before, and they filled the space with an eerie, almost human crying. The massive tiller groaned from side to side. I lit my candle and planted it with molten wax on the tiller and not the deck. The room still smelled of oil, and the planks were slick where my lantern had broken, what seemed like days before but was really only yesterday.

The candle, swinging with the tiller, made grotesquely whirling shadows. The ballast stones rumbled with a sound that made me think of ancient tombs. I sorted through the stack, growing more and more frantic the deeper I went. As I reached the timbers at the bottom, darkly stained with water, I knew the truth.

Larson's book was gone.

Chapter 13
A Tale of Murder

We came out of the fog a mile from shore, and the cliffs of Dover loomed ahead, huge and white, glowing in the sun. Along them lay a coil of smoke, a twisted rope woven from fires at the base and the brink.

"That's the signal," said Dasher. "The revenue knows we're coming."

Crowe wasn't half as calm. "Hard alee!" he shouted, and I watched the cliffs racing sideways past the bowsprit. The *Dragon* turned toward the sea. And again the fog enveloped us.

We sailed to the south for an hour or more, and then to the west. I'd lost all sense of where we were by the time the *Dragon* hove to at Crowe's command. The sails were lowered, and we drifted in the fog.

I sat on the capstan, mulling over my dilemma. If Crowe had the book, he wouldn't wait very long to settle the score between us. At every creak of wood, at every sound I heard, I expected Crowe to come out of the fog. And then I heard the hatch slide open. Footsteps came along the deck, and a man emerged from the gray.

"Lord love me," he said, "I've never eaten a soup any thicker than this."

It was Dasher. I felt almost happy to see him and shifted over to give him room on the capstan. He sat at my side and lit a pipe, and I watched the smoke swirl away to mix with the fog.

"How long will we wait here?" I asked.

"Until it's good and dark," said Dasher.

"And then what?"

"We'll try the other place, of course. And if the revenue's there as well . . ."

From below us came a thump, and then another, muffled by the wood.

Dasher stamped his feet on the deck. He lowered his head and shouted at the planks, "Give it up, you old Haggis!" Then he grinned. "He's looking everywhere for that dead man's book."

He crossed his legs and calmly smoked. Under his breath, he hummed his sad little song.

I stared at him as thoughts spun through my mind. Who had the book if it wasn't Crowe? Was it Dasher himself? Or was the book still among the ballast stones, so deep in the darkness that I'd somehow overlooked it?

"Did you search for it?" I asked him.

"Me?" He shook his head. "I'm not the one who wants it.

Soon as we've got these barrels unloaded, I'm rid of this blasted boat."

"You're going ashore?"

"Like a shot." He swung out his arm with a squeaking of corks and pointed high to the west. "It's over the hills and home for old Dasher. Home to the hearth and the missus. And then, my friend, I'd say you're on your own."

It seemed to me I was on my own already. But Dasher meant this well, and for a moment he leaned so close toward me I felt the corks against my ribs. "Listen," he said. "Make a run for it. When you get your chance, slip away."

"I can't swim," I told him.

"Who can?" he asked. "No, you wait for the boats, you see. They'll come in a fleet, in a regular navy. And if you're quick about it, you can make off with one."

"And what will become of the *Dragon*?"

Dasher shrugged. "The Haggis will do what he has to do. He'll take her out and sink her. But it will break his heart to see her go."

I snorted. "He has no heart."

"He does for the *Dragon*," said Dasher. "And if he has to sink her, he'll kill you for it." Then he told me a story as we drifted there, as the fog grew dark around us.

The *Dragon* had been built as a privateer, and Turner Crowe was the man to sail her, though he wasn't much older than I at the time. The shipwrights made her fast and sleek; armed with a dozen guns, she was set loose to prey like a wolf on the flocks of French ships. But on the day she was launched, there was an accident, and Crowe's own

111

child was crushed below the ship. "Like a smear of jam," said Dasher. "That's what he looked like. A smear of strawberry jam."

I remembered Larson telling me that. Or at least, in his mysterious way, he had hinted of it. *"Death she'll bring you, and I'll promise you that. It's the way of a ship that was christened with blood."*

"In the *Dragon*," said Dasher, "Crowe rounded the Horn and sailed to the Indies. He filled the holds from the battered, smoking wrecks of merchantmen. And he came home a wealthy young man; he bought the *Dragon* for himself."

"He was crazy," said Dasher. "He thought his boy was sort of *in* the ship, a part of the ship. He thought he could hear the little bleeder knocking—tapping—on the hull."

Again we heard thumps below us, and I nearly jolted from the capstan. Dasher laughed. "He went around talking to the boy, at night in his cabin."

"I've seen that," I said. I remembered the way his fingers had touched the bronze of the porthole, lingering at the hinges, as though stroking curls of hair.

"Then he'll never sink her," I said.

"Except to save his neck," said Dasher. "He's felt a touch of the noose already."

"I've seen the scar."

"But do you know what happened?" Dasher fiddled with his pipe as he began another story. "It went like this," he said.

Crowe made a second voyage privateering, in the war against the colonies. Again he filled the hold. But this time, as he ran home in a gale, the *Dragon* strayed too close to

France, and he was taken by a frigate west of Ushant. His crew was imprisoned to wait out the war, but Captain Crowe made a bargain with the French. He smuggled their spies across the Channel, right under the nose of the English.

"How he did it is a mystery," said Dasher. "Some say he hid the men in barrels, others that he rowed them ashore at Sussex. You pays your money and you takes your choice, but I'd guess there was another way. I think the old fox has a lair down below, a secret compartment that he built from the start for his own little stash of plunder." He smiled. "Oh, you have to admire the captain sometimes."

My father, I remembered, had measured the *Dragon*'s holds. Three times he had paced out their length and their breadth, puzzled because the schooner seemed smaller than he'd thought.

"Old Haggis saw peace coming and fled with the *Dragon*," said Dasher. "He set off from Calais with a crew of four to bring one more spy across. But he came into Dover all by himself, standing there at the wheel. When the anchor went down in the harbor, he was the only man aboard. The first thing he did was sluice the decks, and the water came off her red as wine."

"He murdered the crew?" I asked.

"They were French," said Dasher. He put his pipe down and twiddled his mustache. "So the Haggis had the *Dragon*, and once a smuggler, always a smuggler, or so they say. He took all his money and spent it on one enormous run. Tea, my friend: wishy-washy; maskin-pot. He fetched it over from Normandy—so much tea there was just a foot of freeboard left, and that wooden dragon there was up to its eyes in the Channel. But the revenue were waiting—someone tipped them to it—and they found him off the marshes in the moonlight. Every bale and leaf was seized, and the *Dragon* too. Then they took Captain Crowe and they—"

"They hanged him," said I. "The revenue."

"The smugglers!" cried Dasher. "He made such a botch of the run that they hanged him right there. They sat him on a horse and tied his hands behind him. Round goes the noose. Cinch it tight. You never seen a man sit up so straight."

Dasher spread his legs across the capstan. His chin high, his back stiff, he sat as though on horseback.

"Captain Crowe's glaring down at everyone; you've seen the way he glares. His eyes, they burn. All these men down below him, they put the whips to that horse, and out she goes; she bolts. The captain drops like a rock."

Dasher leapt to his feet, his hands at his throat. He tossed his head from side to side in a wild flurry of whiskers and hair. "He's kicking and he's gasping, and his eyes are big as an owl's. He's spinning round and round on the end of that rope, and the branch is bending down to touch his feet to the ground, then jerking him back in the air. Lord, he danced a fine little jig that night." Dasher smiled. "And you know who cut him down? You know who saved him at just that moment?"

"You?" I asked.

"Dashing Tommy Dusker." He laughed. "People talked of that for weeks and months, for miles and miles. You could go from Ramsgate round to Beachy Head, and every second man you'd meet would say, 'Oh, yes, I was there. I saw it happen. Dashing Tommy Dusker riding like a whirlwind to save his captain.' " He glowed as he told me this. "I should have left that rat to die. But oh, it must have been a fantastical sight. Lord love me, I wish I could have stood there and seen it myself. What a picture I must have been. What a trump!"

He sat on the capstan and scratched idly at the corks on his chest. "They'll write about it one day. They'll write books about me, and novels and plays. But it's books that I want. You never die if you're written up in books."

It was nearly dark. At any minute we would set the sails and go on to the end of our journey. And I still didn't know whom to trust, or who it was that held the dead man's book.

"How well do you know Mathew and Harry?" I asked. "I suppose you're all as thick as thieves."

"A funny thing," said Dasher. "Mathew's the one who got torn into halves, but it was Harry that we feared might go all to pieces." He grinned at his own turn of phrase. "Oh, aren't I quick with the words? Mathew would have laughed to hear that one; he was always a man for a joke." He peered at his pipe and poked at the bowl. "Harry's a strange sort of nut. A hard one to crack. First time I saw him was at Pegwell Bay, when I came down with Mathew to get on the boat."

He rambled on, but I hardly listened. At last I'd found a bit of hope, like a candle in the darkness. *"There's only one I can't vouch for,"* the captain had said, and he must have meant Harry. Then surely it was Harry who had come to me with a warning. And maybe, I thought, it was he who had found the book. *"The dead man's secrets. Mind you keep them safe."*

"Harry was a tubman once," Dasher said. "Mathew was in the black guard."

"What do you mean?" I asked.

"Just what I'm saying. A tubman carries the tubs, the barrels. The black guard stands watch in case the revenue show up." He tapped his pipe on the capstan. "There's hardly a man in Kent hasn't been one or the other. When a smuggling run comes in, there's work for everyone."

"It's foul-hearted work," I said.

"It's the free trade," cried Dasher. "And it's all that keeps us going. You'll see for yourself soon enough. The deacons will come to carry the tubs. The masons will come, and the carpenters too. Why, the doctor himself will come for his share."

It was true. I'd seen them written down in Larson's book, farmers and bakers and herdsmen.

"And what do you do," I asked, "when you're not busy smuggling?"

"I rob coaches," said Dasher.

I stiffened beside him. My old suspicions came back in an instant: the sound of his laugh, the way he moved. "How many have you robbed?" I asked.

"Oh, dozens," he said. "Two or three a night sometimes. Why, not a fortnight ago I stopped the coach on the road from Ashford."

I had passed through there with my father on the night he was shot. But any thought I had that Dasher might admit to being the highwayman vanished when he spoke again.

"I got away with pounds and pounds," he boasted. "There was a lady there—a princess, she said she was—a real Bartholomew doll fairly dripping with jewels. I plucked them from her like plums from a pudding. I stuffed my pockets, John, and the law came riding after me. I could hear them coming with horses and hounds. I looked back."

Dasher glanced over his shoulder, into the fog by the bowsprit. "They were only yards behind, trying to follow my trail by the emeralds and pearls that fell from my pockets. But it started raining, and the blasted jewels all melted away. They were only paste; she wasn't a real princess at all."

His story was nothing but fancy. Paste jewels were no softer than real ones; rain would never melt them. But Dasher swept himself up in the tale and seemed to gallop on the capstan with a breeze in his hair.

"I made my escape by the skin of my teeth," he said. "I rode all the way to York, until the horse—my faithful horse—burst its little heart. And even stone-cold dead it kept on going; a quarter mile it ran like that."

He grinned at me. "There! That's a fine tale for my book, don't you think?" He put his pipe in his mouth and took it out again. "The horse was called Clementine."

"That's rubbish," I said.

His happiness faded away; I'd snuffed it out like a candle flame. "You don't believe it?" he asked.

"It's a pack of lies. And so are you," I said. "All you do is make up stories to make yourself seem grand."

There was another thump from the deck below us, but I barely heard it, and Dasher not at all. He stared down at his hands as they fiddled with the pipe.

"You're not a highwayman," I said. "You're nothing but a smuggler."

I meant it cruelly, but Dasher took it as a compliment. "I am that anyway," he said. "Aren't I?"

"And you always were," said I. "The captain told me you were pinned under a box when you were just a boy. Tobacco, was it? Or tea?"

"Something heavy, whatever it was," he said. Then he looked up, grinning again. "But I'll tell you this; I'm the king of all the smugglers! Why, I've killed a dozen men with nothing but my hands."

To my surprise, Captain Crowe shouted out, "And ye'll have your chance to kill one more." He appeared from the stern and not the hold, walking from the fog with a heavy thud of boots.

Dasher stood up from the capstan. "Are we going in?"

"Aye," said Crowe. "Make sail." Then he turned to me. "It's your last chance, Mr. Spencer. Will you be giving me that book, then?"

"I can't," said I.

"Och, ye're a brave lad," he said, "but a fool. It means the end for ye. And the end for the *Dragon* as well." He turned away, shouting at Dasher, calling for Harry. "Jib and mainsail! Arm your lead and cat the anchor. And keep an eye out for that cutter; she won't have gone waltzing awa'."

Chapter 14
THE COAST IS CLEAR

I wasn't asked to work the ship, and I offered no help. The sails went streaming up, and the *Dragon* gathered way. Dasher and Harry together could hardly hoist the anchor from its bed. Long before they had it hanging at the cathead, we were clear of the fog and fetching England on a reach.

The moon was but a sliver, like the white of a thumbnail, yet Crowe cursed its light. All three of the men watched for the cutter to come out of the fog, or out from the shadows of shore. But none watched so hard as I. Crowe, in a jacket now, was as black as the land, and his head seemed to float in the night, turning this way, then that, as we sailed down the path of the moon.

Astern the sea was speckled with silver, but ahead it was dark. The scattered lights of a village seemed far away until I saw the pale lines of the cliffs below them and realized we were much closer to land than I'd thought.

The mainsail sheet was eased and the boom swung wide, spilling wind in a flutter of canvas. One by one the village lights vanished as the cliff rose high above us.

Captain Crowe fumbled below his jacket. "There's no waiting any longer," said he, and pulled a pistol from his waist. He cocked the hammer. He swung out his arm and pointed the thing at me. "Turn around," he told me. I felt a rush of fear until I saw it had no barrel.

He snapped at me. "Turn around, I telt ye. The flash will blind ye otherwise. Look for an answer from shore."

I heard the click of the hammer. A sharp blue light glared against the rigging and the rail. And a moment later, high on the cliff not half a mile ahead, I saw a ball of gold as a lantern was opened and swung in a lazy arc.

It took me back in an instant to the wreck of the *Isle of Skye*. Mysterious lights on a hazardous shore; the same awful thrill of danger and excitement. But then, I had thought the lights were leading me to safety, and this one meant only peril. I watched the light but did not speak.

Then Dasher shouted. "There!" he cried. "The coast is clear."

Crowe, in the moonlight, smiled. As well he might, I thought. Despite myself, I had to admire a man who could sail circles in a blinding fog, then come from it hours later within half a mile of the place he sought. My father had measured Crowe's skills right to the penny, though when it came to gauging character, he'd been abysmal.

The captain put his pistol away and turned the *Dragon* to follow the shore. Whoever it was that stood on the cliff showed us the lantern in brief little flashes. And soon the *Dragon* swung toward it.

"We're on the spot," said Crowe. "Now tak' your soundings, Dasher. And sing out when it's sand that ye're finding."

Dasher went to the weather chains with his coil of line and his lead weight filled at the bottom with tallow. He braced his feet, and when he swung the lead before him the splash it made—in our silent world—was as loud as the fall of a cannon shot. The line sizzled from his hand, the bits of leather and linen that marked the fathoms flying from his fingers like dark little birds.

He knew what he was doing. As the lead hit bottom the line fell straight, and he gauged the depth by the feel of the leather markings. "By the deep twelve," he called, already coiling the line. When the lead came dripping from the water, he touched the tallow at its base. And finding it bare, he called, "Rock on the bottom."

Again he swung the lead, then gathered it smartly in. "Ten fathoms. Rock bottom."

The sound of his chanting was all I heard. His depths, in the same monotonous voice, came ever more quickly as we closed with the shore.

When he called, "Deep six," Crowe turned the wheel. The soundings went deeper, then shallow again. "Shells on the bottom," said Dasher, feeling the tallow, and we turned to the west. The captain, I saw, was following a chart that he kept in his mind, one he knew so well that he could go blindly across it, the way old Mrs. Pye navigated through the corridors of the Baskerville.

"Five fathoms," called Dasher. "By the deep four." He chanted more quickly as the depths grew shallow. "Three fathoms. Three fathoms. Two strips do I see."

"Easy," said Crowe to himself. "Easy there, son." He was talking to the ship, to the spirit of his child.

"Two fathoms," said Dasher. "Sand in the tallow."

"Let go the anchor!" roared Crowe. He kept the wheel steady, then slowly passed the spokes through his hands. "Let go, damn ye! Let go." And to me he said, in a voice that was awful with anger, "Give them a hand, or I'll strangle ye here on the deck."

I went forward, Crowe shouting after me, and found Dasher and Harry wrestling with the anchor. It had snared in the rope meant to lash it in place, all the weight of it hanging by a line no thicker than my thumb. Harry was flat on his stomach, fiddling with knots. Dasher was crying, "Cut it! Cut it, you fool."

"It's your fault," said Harry. "You've put bloody big knots in here."

"Cut it!" screamed Dasher.

Harry pulled out a knife and touched the blade to the line. Strands parted with terrifying pops. They flew away, twisted and wild. And the anchor tumbled down, striking the hull, plunging into the sea.

"Snub up!" shouted Crowe.

Fathoms went out before we stopped the cable with a coil thrown round the bitts. Then it snapped taut, and the *Dragon* jolted, plunged, and finally stopped as the anchor found a bite in the sand.

Dasher turned his back and stepped across the mooring bitts. Harry clutched my arm. "Your book," he whispered urgently, so faint that only I could hear. "I've got the dead man's book."

"Where?" I asked.

His eyes looked past me and widened with sudden fear. His hand fell away from my arm. Captain Crowe came stalking up behind us.

"Who was it made a botchery o' that?" He seethed with anger. "Who's the lubber, then?"

"It was him," said Dasher. He pointed at Harry.

"Ye idiot," shouted Crowe. "We're ower close to the shore, and she'll touch on the tide." I had seen him angry before, but never like this. He seemed ready to kill us all. He looked at the strands of the parted line, at the knife in Harry's hand.

"It wasn't me," said Harry. "Cap'n, please, I—"

Crowe went for him in a blur of fists. I heard the blows and the grunts and squeals. Dasher stood and watched with a wretched look—of horror, I thought, and maybe shame— as they wrestled on the deck. Then the moonlight flashed on the knife blade, and blood flowed out in a stream from the dark bodies locked in a tangle. And only Captain Crowe stood up again.

"You didn't have to do that," said Dasher in a trembling voice. "He was just a poor nut. He was harmless."

"And ye're a coward," said Crowe. "Ye're a slink and a dunghill, and I've half a mind to end ye right here. And if the tide leaves us dry, that I will. I'll tear ye apart with my hands, and I'll have that yellow liver of yours for my supper."

Dasher shook at the force of the words, like a sapling in a gale. But he didn't answer back; he turned his head away. Then Crowe kicked at the corpse. "Throw this rubbish ower the side."

Dasher bobbed his head. "We will," he said. "We'll do it now."

"Damn ye, Dasher, ye'll do it yourself," roared Crowe.

"No," I said. "I'll help." If Harry had put the book in his pocket, I had to find it now.

But Crowe grabbed my shirt and hauled me with him down the deck. "The boats will be here any minute. I want every barrel out within the hour."

He put me to work freeing the hatch covers. He *hurled* me down to the task, then threw at my feet the same knife that a moment ago he'd driven through the heart of a man.

"Cut the lashings," he said. "Or try it on me, if ye've a mind."

I couldn't do it. I couldn't possibly take up that knife and go at him.

He knew it, and I hated him all the more for that. He turned his back on me and went to the halyards. The sails fell in disorderly heaps, in bunches of white like shorn-away feathers. And the *Dragon*, unwinged, rocked in the ground-swell.

With hot tears in my eyes, I worked at the line. The grunting that came from the foredeck, the sounds of heels dragged along planking, filled me with deep despair. Then, for the third time that voyage, I heard a dead man fall into the sea, and with this one went my last hope of ever finding Larson's book.

Captain Crowe did more work with his hands than I did with the knife. He ripped the lashings off and tore the hatches open. All the time, he watched to windward for a sign of the revenue cutter, until the creaking of oars took him to the rail and the smugglers came out of the night. I slid the knife inside my boot and joined him there.

They came in bumboats and longboats, in dinghies and skiffs and flat-bottomed scows. They came in a raggle-taggle navy of dark-dressed men, some of them standing to scull, others sitting to row, half of them bailing and not one of them speaking a word. They emerged from the night like bats from a cave, in a stream without an end, in a sinister, terrible silence. They swarmed up the side and over the rail, down through the hatch to the hold. Fishermen's boots, dainty shoes, big farmers' brogues, all tramped across the deck, clotted with mud. And up came the barrels, seeming to float like balloons, bobbing from hand to hand down the line of men.

It was done with a speed that amazed me, with the rhythm of a morris dance.

Captain Crowe watched the unloading with the same impatience he'd shown in France. No matter how quickly the barrels passed, it had to be quicker. And he beat with a rope end at any man who let them pause for even a moment.

Then up from below came Dasher. I saw him and I gasped.

Underneath his corks was the bright red coat of my high-wayman. On his head was the same broad hat, now with a neat round hole in the brim, where my shot must have passed right through it. Again he was decked out in pistols; from every part of him poked a barrel or a grip. He had a powder horn around his neck, two bags of shot hanging from his belt. Even with his corks, he would sink like a stone if he fell in the water.

I grabbed the tail of his coat as he passed. I wrenched him to a stop. "It *was* you," I cried.

In the look he gave me, every bit of my trust melted away like his fanciful jewels. There was no friendliness there, no warmth or kindness at all. "Get your hands off me," he said.

I held him tighter than ever. "You held up the coach at Alkham."

"So what if I did?" said he. "I've got seven children, and every one a horror. But I had to put food in their mouths, didn't I? After the *Dragon* was seized, there was no smuggling at all, so what choice did I have? Well, I thought if Dick Turpin could rob a stagecoach, so could I. He was a thief and a fool, a butcher's boy."

"You shot my father!" I cried.

"But did I kill him?" asked Dasher.

"You tried to!"

"I harmed no one," he said. "I only robbed the rich to feed the poor, which happened to be myself."

"And it was because of that," I said, "that we went to the Baskerville. It was because of that we met Captain Crowe, and because of that I'll lose the ship and the cargo and everything."

"Are you trying to say it's all my fault?" asked Dasher. He tugged at his coat. "Because it seems to me you were keen on this yourself. Until it turned against you, anyway. Maybe you saw profit in it; I don't know. Adventure, maybe only that. But it was you that said, 'Let's go to France.' Remember that."

He was right. I had my share of the blame. I let go of his coat, and he shook it straight. "But why did you do it?" I asked. "Can you just tell me that?"

Suddenly he looked truly sad for the first time since I'd met him. He scratched at his pathetic suit of corks. "I'm a sheepherder," he said. "That's what I do. I poke sheep around the hills all day. I know you think I'm a reckless cove, but that's the truth. And your blasted coach was the only one I ever robbed. I'll earn tonight a month's wages, so you stay out of my way, you hear? Things are different now. You keep to yourself and it will go all right in the end."

I didn't know what he meant, and he gave me no time to ask. He whirled on his heel and left. He went at a run, then slowed to a swaggering walk. He leapt to the cabin top, up to the foresail boom. And he stood there, a hand on the halyard, a hand on his hip, grinning down at the men on the deck.

"I'm here, boys," said he. It was the old Dasher again, bright with his boyish charm, and I was surprised to find that I could hate a man and like him as well.

"I've done it," he said. "I'm back from France with more spirits than ever haunted a castle. Flying the flag of the heart of oak, dodging the cutters of the revenue."

Not a man paid him the slightest attention. But Dasher stood atop the furled sail and rambled on, full of boasts and deeds. "I outsailed a dead man," he proclaimed. "I swindled the French and outfoxed the navy. Five we left, and only three came back."

A man laughed, and then another, and despite myself I felt awfully sorry for Dasher. "You might give us a hand, Tommy," said one of the smugglers.

Dasher seemed not to notice. He let go of the halyard and went teetering to the middle of the boom. "I'm coming ashore with you. I'll be leading you home. And one day you'll be telling your children that you were there for the run of the *Dragon,* when Dashing Tommy Dusker led the way to safety."

He raised his hand in a fist. "Lads!" he cried. And then he stopped. He froze there, high above us, like a statue of a hero. But slowly his arm came down, and he stared toward the shore with a look of fear. "He's coming," he said.

The revenue, I thought. I spun round. But all I saw was a little boat, with one man rowing and another in the stern. It was a big man who sat there, with a face that seemed to shine.

"Burton!" said Dasher.

A whisper ran through the ship. "It's Burton," said someone. "Burton's coming," said another.

The boat bumped against the hull. And over the rail came a man in fine clothes, with white frills of lace at his collars and cuffs, a watch fob swinging, and a silver-tipped stick in his hand. He stepped to the deck with shoes that were delicate and clean, as though someone had carried him above the mud and the water. His skin was so scrubbed that it sparkled, while his face had the round and pinkish look of a prize pig at the market.

I couldn't help staring; everyone did, even Crowe at the hatch and Dasher on the boom. This was the man Father cursed and hated so, the one he blamed for bringing us close to ruin. On the stained deck of the battered *Dragon*, surrounded by dark-dressed men, Burton was like a single glittering sovereign in a purse full of tarnished pennies.

His stick tapped on the deck. His hands folded across it. Then the fingers of one tugged at the frilly cuff of the other.

The men stood and watched him. Some held barrels and others didn't, but they all breathed hard from their work. Burton stepped up to the nearest one, a strong young man with a farmer's build.

"What's your name?" asked Burton. His voice was soft and polite.

"Jimmy Rivers, sir."

Burton smiled. "Where are you from, Mr. Rivers?"

"East Bottom, sir," the man said proudly. He returned Burton's smile with a grin.

"Any children?"

"Two, sir."

Burton nodded. "And pray tell me," said he, in the same gentle tone, "do you always stand about as idle as a post?" The stick rolled through his fingers. "Hmmm? Are you really such a lazy dullard as you seem to be?"

The grin dropped from the man's face like a theatrical mask. In its place came a look of fear as Burton's hands drew apart, and out from his stick, glinting in the moonlight, came the long, wicked blade of a sword.

In a moment it was done. The young farmer never made a sound as the blade went in through his ribs. He folded up on the deck, and Burton—as casually as he pleased—took out a handkerchief to wipe the blood from his sword.

"I detest idle hands," said he.

The men went to work with the fever of dogs in a harness. They closed up the gap where the farmer had stood, and the barrels passed from hand to hand in a fearful silence. Only Dasher spoke. From his perch atop the boom, he shouted down at the deck. "Back to work, you shiftless lot. I want these barrels off the boat, or it's me you'll answer to the next time."

Burton slid the sword back inside his stick. His voice was as calm as before. "Captain Crowe. A word with you, please."

The *Dragon* touched the bottom then. It was little more than a bump as the schooner dipped in a swell that was deeper than the others, and no one but I seemed to notice. Captain Crowe, busy with his rope end, came through the smugglers and stood before Burton.

I moved toward the rail.

Burton turned the captain aside. "You've done rather well," he said, then glanced pointedly toward me. "No trouble aboard?"

"Och, no trouble at a'."

"Good," said Burton. "I went up to Canterbury. I had

130

a—" He waved a lacy hand. "A *word*, shall we say, with the constabulary about that Captain Dawson up there."

I had no doubt what this meant. *"Poor Captain Dawson was overtaken by thieves on his way from London,"* Father had written me. Only through his death had Crowe come to command the *Dragon*. Now I understood the power in this smuggling gang, and the reason for Father's hatred. In a moment, I thought, Burton would turn to me, and I would see again that sword drawn from his stick.

I backed away.

Again the *Dragon* touched. I quickened my pace. I moved to the rail and slipped over the side. If I got to shore, I thought, if I found the revenue men, I might bring them back before the *Dragon* could sail. With the tide running out, she'd be held fast on the bottom for an hour at least. But before my head had even dropped below the bulwark, I heard Dasher shout, "Wait there, John!" And then Captain Crowe himself roared out, "Stop!"

I slid down the curve of the hull, into a skiff where a man gaped at me from the stern sheets. I shoved him aside and leapt to the next boat, and on to the next, from gunwale to thwart as they rocked and pitched below me.

"Stop!" shouted Captain Crowe again. I saw his shaggy gray shape at the rail. He swore. "After him, Dasher!"

Then Burton's calm voice chilled me right to the bone. "And Dasher," he said, "if the boy gets away, it is *I* you will answer to."

The *Dragon* hit for a third time, harder than ever. I heard the blow shiver through the masts and the rigging. Dark, flitting forms vaulted over the rail, and I raced for the last of the boats, a tiny clinkered dinghy. I fumbled with the line and cast off; I threw myself down at the oars.

Behind me came a band of men, and Dasher was in the lead.

Chapter 15
THE BLACK GUARD

Dasher moved as if he were dancing, leaping high, bounding from boat to boat.

"Ten guineas!" roared Crowe. "Ten guineas for the man who brings me the ugsome head o' that swine."

It was at least a quarter mile to shore, and I rowed faster than I'd ever rowed before. The little boat bounced along, veering madly in the swell, shipping water bow and stern. There were other boats shuttling barrels to shore, and I passed them far to leeward as my little craft wandered down the wind.

The *Dragon* grew indistinct behind me, her hull and masts black against the moon. But a froth of white glimmered in the bulk of her shape, and I knew at least one boat was coming after me. I bent to the oars until my entire body ached, too frightened to glance even once over my shoulder.

I hit the beach so suddenly that I tumbled backward from the thwart. And when I finally scrambled over the bow, oozing mud waited for me. It sucked at my feet and dragged me down, and I plodded more than I ran.

I heard a crunch of wood and looked back as Dasher leapt from a boat he'd beached beside mine. His legs were longer and he waded easily up through the mud, while for me each step was a struggle.

"Wait!" he shouted. "Wait. I can help you."

Once I might have listened, but now I had no trust in him at all. I carried on until the mud gave way to the hard, smooth rock of shingle, and I raced up the beach with Dasher behind me. After days at sea, the land made me dizzy. I reeled, but I was free, I thought; at last I was safe. Then I looked up at the cliffs. They rose impossibly high, all craggy and worn by the sea and the wind. I could no more climb them than hope to fly to the top, and I hesitated for a moment. Turn north or turn south: My life could hang on the decision I made.

To the north were the smugglers. They formed a long line across the beach, from the sea to the cliffs. In the dim glow of moonlight I saw them standing—Dasher's black guard, fifty men or more, each with a stick or a cudgel. And up the line, bent under the weight of the barrels, staggered a dozen more. When they reached the bluff and put their barrels in a pile, they turned and started back for more. Others took them on from there, up a path along the cliffs, lined again by the men of Dasher's black guard.

To the south the cliff stretched on forever, and the beach came up to meet it. Surf broke right against the base—a line of breakers I could not hope to cross.

Dasher gained the shingle and stopped there at the edge

of the mud. He went to one side and then the other, trying to find me in the shadows at the base of the cliff.

"John!" he shouted. "John, where are you?" Then he pulled off his corks, cast them down, and went at a sprint to the south.

I went north. I walked up to the smugglers and slipped in among them. No one challenged me; no one spoke at all. I took a barrel from the heap and fell in place with the men going up the cliff.

They carried two each, in slings that let the barrels hang down their backs and their chests. Even boys my own age carried two barrels this way. But the one weighed me down, and I was pleased to find myself in the wake of a fat man who wheezed like a tired old horse. Up we went as others came down, while the guard stood watch on the trail.

The path twisted back on itself and rose up again. And the line seemed to vanish ahead. Each man came to a certain point on the trail and disappeared, as though one by one—like lemmings—the smugglers were stepping from the edge of the cliff.

With a start, I heard Dasher below me. I glanced over the edge and saw him, a pistol in his hand. He was shouting my name. "John!" he cried. "John Spencer!" And then, half winded, he asked the men around him, "Have you seen a boy dressed like a sailor? Has a boy gone by?"

I felt every eye on my back but didn't look up. I pressed myself against the heels of the fat man and cursed him now for slowing me down. I heard Dasher start up the trail. There were oaths and grunts as he forced his way through.

A yard ahead the fat man disappeared. In the blink of an

eye he was gone. And right after him, I slipped into utter darkness. Into the mouth of a tunnel.

It closed around me, hot with the breath and the sweat of the smugglers, and thick with a stench of burning oil. But even in the darkness I could see the feet of the man ahead of me, for an eerie light rose from the broken shells covering the floor. In the shards that crunched under our shoes was held the sea's phosphorescence, a pale and shimmering green. The tramp of the smugglers' boots, the slosh of the brandy, echoed through the space with a sound like surf on a beach.

The tunnel slanted down, so I felt myself pulled by the weight of my load, pushed by a breeze that blew from behind. Then it sharply turned and rose at a steeper angle; lanterns set in the wall cast thin little blades of gold. And in this smoky haze was lit the line of wretched men, bent and coughing as they trudged along.

Dasher's shouts came louder, closer. But each time I tried to get past the fat man, it was only to meet other men coming down. Someone cuffed me on the ears and told me roughly, "Get back in line." My fingers burned where they held the barrel; my arms felt stretched to twice their length.

I must have gone half a mile before I felt a gust of air, as the tunnel turned once more to open at a storeroom. It was an enormous cellar built of stone, without a window anywhere. In a near corner was a staircase. In the far wall, an open door led to a ramp that climbed steeply to a village street, and the smoke from the tunnel swirled out in coils of gray. At the top was a wagon, with a pair of patient horses and a dozen men around it.

Dasher's shouts came close behind me, loud and short of breath. "The boy!" he cried. "Stop the boy."

I followed the fat man toward the door. He put his barrels down on the cellar floor, but I kept on going. Another moment would get me free from there; fifty paces would take me to a road. I passed through the door and started up.

Hands closed on my shoulder, pulling me back. "Where do you think you're off to?"

It was the fat man. He pulled the barrel from my arms and set it down with his. "Others take them up," he said. "You go back for another."

A suspicious look came to his face. He bent toward me, his hand on my collar. "Who are you?" he asked. "I've never seen you before."

Dasher shouted, "Stop the boy!"

I wrenched away as Dasher came hurtling from the tunnel mouth. I ran for the door, but the guards were coming down. I wheeled away and raced for the staircase. I pounded up the wooden steps, and others came behind me.

At the top was a hallway, wooden-floored, even darker than the smugglers' tunnel. Not the faintest glimmer of light showed me which way I should go. With my back pressed to the wall, I shuffled along until I came to a corner, and around it to another flight of stairs set deep in a narrow doorway, rising to a second floor. But the boards creaked horribly under my weight, and I dared not make another sound. I crouched at the bottom and waited.

Dasher was first up the steps from the cellar. His voice boomed down the hall. "Where are you?" And then, in a whisper, "Lord love me, I don't like the darkness."

Others thundered up behind him, and then the glow of lanterns spread along the walls, painting them yellow and gold. I could hear the smugglers breathing. Their boots tapped and scuffed on the floor. They were sure to find me.

But Dasher cried, "This way!" And I could hear that they took the wrong turn at the top of the stairs.

For a long time I crouched there, listening. A door opened, and then another. The footsteps stopped, but the voices didn't, and I crept from my doorway and poked my head round the corner. At the end of the hall was a kitchen, and there the smugglers stood in a half circle, their backs toward me as they huddled at a counter. Halfway between us, on the far side of the hall, an open door spilled the lanterns' light onto a street.

I wanted to run, but I dared not do it. Instead I crept along, close to the wall to keep the floorboards from squeaking. I moved slowly but steadily. I made no sound at all, and I kept my eyes on the smugglers.

I was only yards from the door when a voice called out from the kitchen. It was reedy and old, a woman's voice.

"Is that you, Flem?"

I was too surprised to move. The huddle of men broke open, and old Mrs. Pye came out from behind them. "Fleming?" she asked in that broken voice. "Is that you, Fleming? Is that you at last?"

She tottered toward me, smiling grotesquely, preening her thin bits of hair.

I would never have guessed I'd come back to the Baskerville Inn. But as I stood there, utterly helpless, I felt the same waft of air through the tunnel that I'd felt here what seemed like a lifetime ago. I remembered the smell that came with it, the one of the sea.

"My darling," said Mrs. Pye. "At last you've come home."

It was Dasher who spoke. "It isn't Fleming, you old dishclout. It's a boy," said he. "An informer. A rat of a boy."

He barged past her and grabbed me. The others came after, and the old woman spun and staggered along, groping for the wall. If the smugglers had had their way, they would have killed me right there; they would have bashed me to death with the clubs they carried. But Dasher said, "No! He's mine. I've waited long for this." And he hauled me out through the door, dragging me into the street.

"I'll kill him!" he shouted. "I'll shoot him down like the dog that he is."

Dasher pulled me and pushed me to the banks of a little stream. He whirled me round, and his hands filled with pistols. "I'll blow his head off!" he shouted. "I'll put a ball through his heart."

And he fired the guns.

What they say is true: Your life flashes before you. But mine was a short little life, and I saw myself grow in an instant from a baby to a boy. I saw myself on my father's shoulders with my hands pulling at his hair. I saw my mother's deathbed and her horrid, twisted face. I saw the *Isle of Skye,* and then Mary's kind face, her sweet smile. And last I saw the towering waves of the Tombstones. I felt them close over me as cold as ice, and I tumbled backward into the rushing stream.

Chapter 16
A GANG OF MEN

The water was fast and bubbly, not salty at all. It shocked me with its coldness and its blackness, as deep as all eternity. I seemed to fall forever, though the stream was not much more than a foot in depth.

Dasher hauled me out. He slid me up the grassy slope, on my back, until I lay with only my legs in the water. He looked worried; I thought he might be crying.

"You're all right, aren't you?" he whispered.

"I don't know," I told him.

"Sure you are." He grinned. Then he lifted his head and shouted back at the inn. "Still alive! Damn me, the boy's still alive." And he pulled another two pistols out of his belt.

They were bright with gold that flashed in his hands. Larson's pistols. He aimed them down and cocked the hammers.

"No," I said. "Please."

"It's all right," he told me. "They're not loaded. Not a one of them's loaded." And he fired them both. "That will show you!" he shouted fiercely. "That's you done for!" He pulled pistols from his belt and his bandolier; he stuffed them back as the smoke still swirled from the barrels. With each shot, a shout: "Take that, you devil. Take that, you rogue!" Then he winked at me. "Oh, isn't this grand?"

He put on quite a show for the smugglers, who hadn't moved from the doors of the inn. And he reveled in the noise and the smell of the powder, in the sudden flare of orange that lit him each time against the black of the sky. But there were still half a dozen pistols untouched in his belt when the smugglers called out and told him to stop. "They'll hear you in Ashford," they shouted. "You'll have the whole preventive here."

Dasher put his guns away. "I'll just cut his throat, then," he said, and came down to crouch beside me.

I was nearly deafened, and half blinded by the glare and the smoke. But I wasn't hurt at all, and I realized now why my father had come away with only a burn on his coat.

"I couldn't harm you," said Dasher. "I could never hurt a soul." He got me sitting on the bank; he told me to rest for a while. "Then slip away to London. You'll get the coach at St. Vincent."

"London?" I said. "And leave the *Dragon* with Captain Crowe?" I shook my head. "My father's fortune is in that ship."

"It's lost at any rate," said Dasher.

We heard voices coming nearer, and lantern light flashed across the ground. Dasher thrust his head up over the banks and shouted out, "You lot stay where you are! I'll just turn out his pockets!" Then he bent to me again. "I have to go," he said. "But here, take this."

He reached inside his coat and pulled out a dark little bundle. I stared in astonishment at Larson's oil-skinned packet. "I found this on Harry," Dasher said. "Lord knows how he got it. I told Captain Crowe not to trust that one." He pressed the envelope into my hands. "Take it to London. Straight to the Old Bailey. Find one of those gents with a cauliflower on his head—you know those white wigs they wear. Put that straight in his hands and tell him, 'Here you go, sir. Here's a present from Dashing Tommy Dusker.'" He chuckled. "I guess that will bring an end to old Haggis. And to a whole lot of others who put on the airs when they see me."

"Thank you," I said.

"But one other thing." He looked at me with his rakish grin. "Go through it yourself. Look for my name in there. And make sure that—"

"I'll cut it out," I promised. "Or I'll blotch it, or something."

"No," he said. "If you see I'm *not* there, will you write me in? Will you do that, John?"

It was the strangest thing I'd ever been asked, but of course it was just what he'd want. *"There'll come a day you'll hear of me,"* he'd said. *"They might have to hang me first, but hear of me you will."*

"Promise?" he asked.

"I promise," I told him.

Dasher gave me a clap on the shoulder, then left me there at the stream. He climbed up the bank and posed at the top for a moment, with the breeze in his coat. Then he swaggered off toward the Baskerville, already boasting of his deed. "You should have seen the way he squirmed. Should have heard him beg."

I lay hiding for a long time, until the moon was nearly down. But the little village never fell silent. Wagons rumbled over the bridge; the inn door opened and closed. When I crawled up the bank and peered over the edge, I saw a gilded old hearse draw up at the inn and go off with a load of barrels. And behind it, to my chagrin, came the coach I'd ridden in with Father, the same driver hopping down from his seat to open the doors for the tubmen. It was no wonder, I thought, that he'd found his way to the Baskerville. No wonder he'd known poor Mrs. Pye.

I knew Dasher was right. The *Dragon* might be lost already, and with her my father's fortune. But I couldn't brave the thought of facing Father as I told him how I'd left the ship with Captain Crowe. He'd put all his trust in me alone, and I couldn't let him know how badly I had failed. I watched the moon, and when it touched the trees I started down the stream. Back toward the sea.

I waded through the water, which tumbled along, over shelves of rock, going steadily down and always faster. It had worn a gully into the cliffs, but in places it fell a fathom straight, in a foaming, roaring fury. I slid and splashed and stumbled, with one hand to keep my balance, one to hold Larson's packet safe within my shirt. And I slipped down past the edge of a cataract.

Right into the arms of a man.

He lunged up from the darkness, from the side of the stream where it pooled below the falls. He forced my face down and held me there, his knee on my back, with the water almost touching my nose. "And where are you off to?" he asked.

I didn't answer quickly enough. He plunged my head under the surface, and I heard the roar from the falls as I struggled against him. His hand in my hair, he pulled me up again. "Where?" he shouted.

I gasped for breath. "The *Dragon*," I said. "Back to the *Dragon*."

"I thought as much," said he. "But you'll not be doing that, my boy."

With a twist of my arm he rolled me onto my back, and I stared up at a man in a mud-dabbled uniform. An officer's clothes. I was so shocked, so pleased, that I blurted out, "Good God! The revenue!"

"Yes," he said, and shook me. "And what's your name? Who are you, boy?"

"Spencer," I said. "John Spencer. And I know where the smugglers are. I can take you there."

He laughed. "You hear that? The boy's a turncoat."

From the bushes and the rocks came a gang of men. They all wore the same blue jackets, dark neckerchiefs, and battered hats with ribbons at the crowns. They filled the space at the bottom of the falls.

"Up you get," the officer said. "You're coming along with us."

"Wait!" I cried. "I'm not a smuggler."

"Course you're not." He dragged me to my feet. "You lot are all the same. No one's a smuggler when the revenue's there."

"It's true," I said. "Just listen. I can take you where they are."

"And where is that?"

"The Baskerville," said I.

He snorted. "That's half a mile from the sea."

"There's a tunnel," I said. "It comes out at the inn."

I was hardly aware that we'd been shouting over the noise of the falls. But now the beating water was all I heard as the revenue men stared at me in astonishment.

"I have a book." I fished the packet from my shirt. "All their names—"

"Damn your book," the officer said. He shoved my hand rudely away. "It's a fine story, boy, a tunnel up from the sea. We'll just see about that. We'll see if it's true."

"I have to get to the *Dragon*," I said.

"And send us off on a goose chase? I think not, my boy." He took my arm and hauled me up the slope. "You'll come along with us, you will."

There were more than a dozen men; I had no choice but to lead them back. Each one carried a cutlass, and most had a pistol or two. They pulled them out and examined the flints, and in the darkness it was a sinister thing to see.

The officer sent two men down to the beach, to watch for any smugglers who might come from the tunnel. Then he told me, "Show us the way. And for your own sake, boy, we'd best find the smugglers there."

I put the packet back in my shirt and led them, as fast as I could, up through the gully and over the ground at the top. They followed behind in a line, grunting up the steepest parts, their cutlasses clanging on stones. And then the Baskerville rose above us, black and hulking, with not a single bit of light in any of its windows.

"Empty," said the officer. "I might have guessed as much."

"They're in the cellar," I said. "They're taking the barrels out to the street." And even as I spoke, the hearse came jangling back down the road, its four black horses all in a run.

"They'll put barrels in there," said I. "Brandy straight from France."

We circled the inn and came out at its front. We looked in through the open doors to the hazy glow of the lantern-lit cellar. The hearse stood outside, its rear doors open. Around it lounged the black guard. And in the pool of golden light that came through the door, I saw Burton himself with his stick and his fine-looking clothes.

"There," I said, and pointed. "That's Burton, the head of it all."

"So it is," the officer said. "I'll tell you, boy, I've waited years for this. Years and years I've waited."

He spread his men out in an arc, to the left and the right, by hedgerows and trees. And for a long, long moment we waited.

I said, "There's a woman in there. Old Mrs. Pye. She's —"

"Blind?" he asked. "Sure, we all know Sally Pye. She won't be harmed, boy. No fear about that."

He turned his head to look at me. "You can stay right here," he said.

"No," I said. "I can't. They nearly killed me; they nearly drove my father from his business. I have to go with you. I have to."

"You're a brave lad." He put his cutlass into my hand. "Ready?" he asked.

I nodded.

He stood, and I stood beside him. He raised his hand in the air, and I lifted the sword. We started forward at a walk and, yards from the inn, broke into a run.

He shouted out, "Hold there! Hold in the name of the king!"

The smugglers, like rats caught in daylight, scurried for the cellar. They dropped the barrels on the ground; they trampled each other in a rush to escape.

I saw bright flashes of powder, and a crackle of gunfire burst through the night. I hurdled a ditch, crossed over the road, then raced past the hearse and down the ramp to the cellar.

It was madness inside. Men were locked into pairs, struggling with fists or with swords. The blue jackets of the revenue men were lost in the mass of smugglers. A pistol shot banged in my ear; a hand clamped on my shoulder. I whirled round.

And there stood Burton, his stick in his hand.

"You!" he said. "So this is your doing, is it?"

"Yes," said I. Just to see him standing there gave me

shivers that knocked my knees together. Never had I felt such fear of a man, but neither such hatred.

"You're nothing but a pup," he said, as calmly as before. "A meddling little dog that's hardly worth my trouble."

He spun his stick in an arc past his knees. It seemed to fly from his hand; I saw it sail high through the cellar, then heard it clatter against the ceiling. But it was only the sheath he'd cast away. The sword was still in his hand, and it glinted in the light of the lanterns.

I raised the cutlass. He knocked it aside. I took a step back, and he came after me.

"Come, come," he said. "You'll have to do better than that."

I wasn't a fencer. I'd never used a sword. Again I raised the cutlass; again he knocked it away.

I went backward into the storm of swirling men, a step at a time, right through the mass of them. And Burton came steadily on. He lunged at me and put a nick in my sleeve. He lunged again, and I twisted aside with the blade passing an inch from my heart.

The cellar was thick with dust and a clamor of voices. The heat filled my eyes with sweat. The hilt of the cutlass slithered in my fingers as I tried to parry Burton's thrusts.

He swept the blade aside. He came forward with a smile on his face, poking at me like a child at a cat. Then he surprised me with a slashing cut that jangled off the cutlass guard. And when I stepped back I felt my shoulders touch the wall. I could move no farther.

"A pathetic little fight," he said. "It's a sorry ending for you, boy."

He attacked with the point of the sword. He put all his weight into that lunge, and I watched with a dreamlike terror as the point tore through my shirt.

I didn't feel the blade go in. I heard Burton grunt, and it was as though he had hit me with his fist instead. The blow slammed against my stomach with a solid thud, and when he drew his arm away, the sword slipped from his hand and hung there, sagging from my stomach.

Unbalanced, Burton staggered back. I gripped the cutlass with both my hands, swung it up, and swung it down. It twisted in my palms, and I struck him with the flat of the blade, on his jaw and neck. But the blow knocked him to the floor, facefirst into the dust and the blood. And before I could strike him again, the revenue officer threw himself between us. He came at a rush from the mass of men and stopped my hand with his.

"Wait!" he cried. "There's a trophy for the hangman."

Then again I saw Burton's sword poking from my stomach. And my knees gave way, and I sank down against the wall.

The fighting had ended, leaving the cellar littered with bodies. The smugglers were being led from the cellar in groups of three and four. A dozen more came shuffling out of the tunnel, with revenue men herding them on.

The officer used his neckerchief to bind Burton's hands at the wrists. He tightened the knot until Burton groaned.

"Shut up," growled the officer. "One more sound—a single word—and I'll slit your throat." He grinned. "Just ask me if I won't."

Burton made no sound at all.

The officer crawled toward me. "Don't move," he said. "Let's have a look at you there."

"I don't *feel* hurt," I said.

"It's the shock," he told me. "Now lie quiet, boy."

Chapter 17
A JERKIN OF CORKS

The revenue officer opened my shirt. He probed with his fingers down the blade of the sword, but I couldn't feel his movements at all. Then he pinched the blade in his hand and yanked it free. And with it, skewered on its tip, came Larson's oilskin packet.

"There's a bit of luck," he said, and plucked the packet from the sword. "Look at that, boy."

He passed it to me, and I opened it. The point had pierced the envelope and embedded itself in Larson's book. It was all that had saved me.

"Is that your book?" he asked. "The smugglers' names?"

I nodded.

"It will have to go to London."

He reached out to take it, but I held it away. I had made a promise to Dasher, and I meant to keep it before I gave the book to anyone else. "I could take it there myself," I said.

"And why not?" said he. "You're going directly to London, are you?"

"As fast as I can."

It was the truth, but not entirely so. Yes, I would go to London as quickly as possible. But first I had to see to the *Dragon*. First I had to deal with Captain Crowe.

The revenue officer hauled Burton to his feet. For a moment my eyes met the smuggler's, and I saw there the same look a mouse would see in those of a cat about to spring upon it.

"You've lost the ship," said Burton. "You know that, don't you? The ship and the cargo and all that you have. What a fine job you've done, to lose so much so fast."

The officer struck him on the mouth, and blood bubbled at Burton's lips. "Shut up, I told you!" the officer said. And then, to me, "Are you coming along?"

I said, "I'd like to sit for a while."

"I understand." He tugged viciously at Burton's arms and sent him staggering toward the door. "I owe you a debt, boy," he said. "All of England owes you a debt."

I watched him go through the door. Then I climbed to my feet and started off down the tunnel.

I ran down its length in the glow of the lanterns, in the shine of the shells, out through the mouth and down to the sand. A faint glimmer of starlight was enough to show me that the beach was deserted. There was not a soul to be seen, not a smuggler or revenue man. Yet the *Dragon* was right where I'd left her, hulking and huge, barely afloat on the rising tide.

It seemed that Captain Crowe had abandoned the ship.

Perhaps he had fled at the sight of the revenue, leaving her stuck in the mud, empty of all but the wool. If I could get to the *Dragon*, I thought, I still might save her. Even alone, I could raise enough sail to take her back to the Downs. *"A man and a boy can handle a schooner,"* the captain had told me.

Soon I discovered that my dinghy was gone, as was the boat that Dasher had used. The whole little fleet seemed to have vanished, though it shouldn't have surprised me. Likely it was the first thing the smugglers did, for an empty boat in the morning would be a sure sign to the revenue that work had been done in the moonlight. But my discovery left me disheartened.

As I plodded along the beach, I came to the footprints I'd left in my rush from the schooner, and a thought occurred to me—a desperate last hope. I scuffed through the black stones and the shells at the edge of the mud. I got down on my hands and knees. I crawled and I groped and finally found what I wanted: Dasher's jerkin of corks.

It was loose and bulky on me, but it was the best I could do. I tied the strings as tightly as possible and waded down through the mud, into the sea. The breeze had hauled around to blow softly from the land, but there was no sign of fog, and that pleased me. The thought of losing my way and drifting off to God knew where was enough to start my knees knocking.

The water was bitterly cold, and as it rose to my stomach, my breath came in short little gasps. The jerkin bunched around my arms, and I was chest-deep in the Channel before I felt my feet lift from the bottom. I tipped backward, then forward, and the sensation of floating—so strange to one who'd never learned to swim—filled me with an instant panic. I thrashed and kicked; I clung with a death grip to the jerkin of corks. And round I spun, round and round as I beat the water into froth, nearly screaming from my fright. Then my feet touched the bottom again, and I stood there until I'd gathered myself. I knew I had to get out to the *Dragon*.

Slowly my panic subsided. I found I could move forward as a dog would, by paddling my arms and my feet. I aimed myself toward the schooner, pushed off from the mud, and went forward at a crawl.

The rising tide was stronger than the breeze. I went toward the *Dragon* so slowly that I seemed to make no headway. The groundswell lifted me and dropped me in the troughs, and salt water lapped at my mouth and my nose. Yet each time I looked up, the masts were a little bit taller and the bulk of the hull loomed a bit closer. And I'd gone too far to turn back when I heard the voices come across the sea.

"Cut it," said Crowe. "Cut the damn thing. We'll never need it again."

The *Dragon* wasn't deserted at all.

Soon I saw figures on the foredeck. Crowe and two others. I heard a steady, hammering pulse, and at once I knew they were cutting the anchor cable. So the schooner was floating already, and any moment the men would make sail. I paddled and kicked. And with a pop of threads, and then another, the corks started coming loose from the jerkin.

They floated past me, borne by the breeze. First two or three, then half a dozen, they spun and leapt in the ripples of water. Absurdly, I grabbed for them, and my motions brought others loose. For the first time I felt the sea at the back of my neck. I was starting to sink.

The hammering stopped. I heard the slither of rope as the cable fell from the rail. The *Dragon* turned, slowly at first, and then faster. A pair of boats tied to her stern followed with a jerk and a nod, like goslings behind a goose. The jib went up, and then the mainsail, and the schooner gathered way.

I threw myself forward. I no longer paddled but swam, reaching far out before me, taking handfuls of water, pulling myself through the swell the way a man would climb a cliff. The last of the boats swung toward me, and I reached up and grabbed on to the transom. But I was a moment too late; it pulled from my fingers and slipped away. A cork-filled eddy went behind it.

All alone in that black of sea and sky, I felt the panic returning in a rush. I forced it down and kept on going. The water rose to my chin.

Even now I like to think that the *Dragon* turned to fetch me. I like to think she saw me somehow and tried her best to save me. But it was only Captain Crowe. He had taken the schooner in to shore on a winding, twisting path, and he took her out the same way. He jibed and came back, and the big wooden jaws of the dragon ate through the swells. The teeth were high above me, then buried in the sea. They rose and fell and rose again, then snatched me from the water.

It seemed the greatest bit of luck at first, and I lay resting within the jaws as the water coursed around my legs. Then the *Dragon* turned again, to sail from the lee of the cliffs, and every wave overwhelmed me. The figurehead became my prison, the teeth the bars to hold me in. The bow soared up, then hurtled down, and I was buried in the sea. And the motion that I had loved to watch on the outward journey was now a nightmare sure to drown me.

I shouted for help, with no thought of who might respond. I would have been happy to see Captain Crowe himself come climbing down to haul me out from there. But with the roar that the figurehead made, I was sure no one could hear.

The bowsprit dipped, and half its length was buried in a wave. I rode the dragon's mouth toward the sea and then beneath its surface. The water hit me like a pile driver, and when the schooner lifted, I tumbled back. I slammed against a bulk of wood that trembled and groaned behind me. The schooner threw me forward; the water hurled me back. The wood rattled each time I bashed against it. And I heard a voice in all that racket, a voice as high as a boy's but old as all the hills. "Who's there?" it said. The ship herself, I thought. "Who's there at the mouth of the dragon?"

Up I soared, the schooner climbing from the sea. She rolled and took me down. The water burst through the teeth, slammed against my chest. And the wood gave way behind me. I somersaulted backward in a flood of boiling sea, down through the throat of the dragon, into the hull of the ship.

I lay on a planked floor, staring up at a withered old man who held in his hands a panel of wood. I could look beyond him, right through the bow and the teeth of the dragon.

"Knock me down with a feather!" said he. "Where the devil did you come from, boy?"

I was too surprised to answer. The schooner dipped her bow again, and a blast of water shot through the hole. It poured across the deck and washed me down against the planking and the ribs. The man struggled forward and pressed the panel over the hole. It fit exactly, locking in place, sealing us into darkness.

"And now me candle's gone out," said the man. "Oh, this is the end. This is the bleeding last straw, this is."

I heard him groping round, banging on wood and metal. Then came the tap of a flint, and sparks flew in a flurry from his hands. "You see what you've done?" he said. "You've got me tinder wet. Blast you."

There were more sparks, and then a faint glow, and at last a flame as he held a candle to the tinder. He held it high above him, and the light made a yellow circle on the overhead. His hands were big and pale, his nose enormous. Hair as white as cotton thread grew in thick tufts from his nostrils and his ears. I knew at once that he was the same old man I'd seen lurking on the dock in France, the one who had passed in front of the *Dragon* and never appeared again.

"Who are you?" I said.

"I'm Fleming Pye," said he. "And more's to the point, who are *you*?"

Chapter 18
THE ONLY ONE LEFT

The old man would tell me none of his story until he'd heard every detail of mine. Then he hurled questions at me, beginning each one with a cry of "Tell me this!"

"Tell me this!" he said. "Just what do you plan to do now?"

I shrugged. "I have to get the ship back somehow. They're going to scuttle her for certain."

"Tell me this! How many are up there?"

"Three at least," said I. "Maybe more."

"And that's including Turner Crowe."

"Yes, it is."

"He's a rascal," said Fleming. "He's a wily old eel of a man."

"How do you know him?" I asked.

"Used to sail with him, boy. Until he sold me out to the French. Until he left me to rot in prison."

Fleming mounted the candle on the top of his tinderbox. It skittered all over the deck as the *Dragon* sailed along. And in its dim and hazy light I saw how this hidden space extended down the ship in narrow aisles as cramped as rabbit warrens. This would be the place, I thought, where French spies had waited out their trip to England, emerging from the bow like water rats in the safety of the night.

"I'm the only one left," said Fleming. "There was twenty men sailed with Turner Crowe, when we went privateering. There was sixteen alive in seventy-nine when the French took us on the last day of September, just after dawn. That was the last sunrise I saw for twenty-two years. Now tell me this! You know what I want? The only thing that I want?"

"To kill Captain Crowe," said I.

He laughed. He sat in a crouch in that dank, foul-smelling place, and he laughed until I thought it would shake his old bones apart. "Kill Captain Crowe?" he said. "You can't kill a devil, boy. You can't kill the father of evil."

"What, then?" I asked.

"I want to get home to me woman. She's all I've got left in the world. I've forgotten what me house is like, but I remember me Sally like it was yesterday I saw her."

"Is that Mrs. Pye?" I asked foolishly.

"Sally Pye," he said, and smiled. "Tell me this! Do you know her?"

"I've met her," I said. "She waits for you at the Baskerville Inn."

"Oh, the poor thing," said Fleming. "The poor, simple thing. 'Wait here,' I told her. 'Wait for me here.' And she did, the poor thing." His eyes closed. He combed with his fingers the wiry tufts that grew from his nostrils. "Tell me this! Is she every bit as pretty? Is her hair more gold than gold itself? Is her skin as smooth as porcelain?"

I didn't know what to say. I thought of the haggard old woman going blindly through the inn. And I suppose I waited a moment too long.

Fleming's face, which the smiles had made young again, aged in an instant. "Tell me this!" he said. "Is she all right? Is she well?"

I couldn't bear to tell him the truth, so I shifted the conversation. "We were there," I told him. "We anchored just under the inn."

"I knew it," said he. "I said to myself, 'That's the mud of St. Vincent I'm smelling.' The mud and the apple trees. And I could hear that little brook that bubbles down from the cliffs. But the panel was jammed and I couldn't get it open. It needed a bang. It needed a blow from beyond."

"You could tell all that without a look outside?"

"Why, sure," said he. "I've come to this place a hundred times. There were nights I could stand at the wheel and not see the binnacle. I couldn't see me hands on the spokes, or me feet on the deck, but I could always get back to the Baskerville."

"Could you take us into Dover?" I asked.

"In me sleep," said Fleming.

I had a scheme that seemed too wild to tell him. I watched the candle slide toward the bow, and I asked, "Can we get from here to the lazarette?"

"Of course," he said.

"And could you steer the ship from there?"

The candle slid the other way. Fleming shoved out his foot and stopped it. "Tell me this!" He took the tinderbox in his hands. "Do you want me to take her to the Eastern Docks or the jetty under the castle?"

He led me aft to the lazarette by way of a panel that opened on hinges. He held it ajar until I'd gone through behind him.

"When I close this," he said, "there's no going back. The only way in there is through the dragon's mouth."

"It's all right," I said. "We're not going back."

The sound the panel made was like a tomb being sealed. There was a thud and a dull click of hidden latches. Fleming went before me, guarding the flame of his candle.

In the lazarette, we watched the tiller sliding back and forth. The steering lines hung in lazy curves that snapped taut as the wheel turned above us. I imagined it was Crowe himself steering the ship to her doom. But faintly through the decking came the sound of his bagpipes, a slow and funereal march.

Fleming looked up. In the candlelight he seemed older by centuries. "He played that song when we took the *Sentinelle,* a little brig we stumbled on a hundred miles from St. Helena. He played it as we watched her burn. There was women on there. And children. We took the boats and burned her."

"But you took the people in the boats," I said.

"No. Just the boats." He put his fingers in his ears and stuffed the hair inside them, then turned toward the tiller.

"We'll have to cut the lines," he said. "Have you got a knife?"

"No," I said. Then, "Yes, I do." Crowe had thrown me Harry's knife to cut away the lashings on the hatch. I had put it in my boot. But now, when I searched for it, I found it was gone.

"Never mind," said Fleming. "It's just like Crowe to keep things shabby. He likes his rats' nests, don't he, though? These lines are loose enough we can pull them from the drum."

"And you'll steer with the tiller?" I asked.

"Tell me this!" said he. "Have you heard of Cape da Roca? We had the wheel shot off there. This was seventy-six. Shot clean from the deck. I steered all the way to Gibraltar down here. Three hundred miles it was."

Well, he had been half his age then. But if he thought he could still manage the task, I was willing to let him try. No matter what happened, we'd be no worse off than we were.

"Just give the ropes a heave," said Fleming. "Wait till the helm's amidships."

It wasn't long to wait. The massive tiller groaned across the deck and shivered at the center line. We put our weight on the ropes and stripped them from the drum.

Freed from its lines, the tiller hurtled toward us. The deck tilted so violently that we grabbed at each other for balance and still went staggering down toward the hull. We fell in a heap against the planks. The steering ropes twisted and writhed as someone above us turned the wheel. But the tiller, thrown hard to the side, didn't move at all.

We helped each other up from the deck. Fleming's arms, where I held them, were no thicker than those on a rocking chair.

The tiller was level with his waist, and he leaned across it. Like a man pushing a gate, he walked it across as the rudder banged and rattled. I felt the *Dragon* turn; the deck came quickly level as the schooner gathered way. Water passing by the rudder made the tiller tremble. And poor Fleming trembled with it; from head to toe he was shaken like a puppet.

"Tell me this!" he said. "Do you think you can run up and see if we're on course? Take the candle. And hurry, boy. I'll have her at the jetty before you know it."

I went up through the fo'c's'le, to that strange light of a coming dawn, too faint to give color to anything. Ours was a gray ship on a black sea, and across the darkened deck leapt a thing that gave me a thrill of horror. It looked like an enormous spider scuttling along. It tumbled over the planks on thin, stiff legs, then jumped to the rail and vaulted into the void beyond.

It was only the bagpipes, of course, the captain's green bagpipes. He'd cast them away to tend to a ship that seemed to have a mind of her own. There was no one at her helm, but she kept a steady course toward the land. And try as Crowe might, he would not get her to stray from that.

All the sails were set, but a madman might have trimmed them. The topsail was braced aback; the mainsail was hauled far to windward with a preventer rigged to hold it there. The canvas fluttered and cracked, yet the *Dragon* rushed for the rising sun. Only one of the boats was in tow. The other bobbed far from the stern, and I saw two men at the oars, rowing for all they were worth.

The *Dragon* went with her roar and her spray, as though Crowe could strip every sail from her spars and still she would spite him. He stood all alone at the mainmast, staring up at the billowing sail. Two halyards held it in place, one to the peak of the gaff and one to its throat, and already he'd thrown off the coiled ropes from their belaying pins. Just a hitch or two at either one held the sail in place, and the ropes lay in ragged piles that stretched and shifted with the *Dragon*'s roll.

As I watched, Crowe pulled the pin to let the peak go free. The big wooden gaff dropped toward the mast, hauling the rope up through its blocks. The line snapped and twitched around his feet, leaping from the deck in kinks and coils; half the rope vanished in a moment, shrieking through the pulleys. The top half of the mainsail collapsed, but still the *Dragon* stayed on her course. Crowe kicked at the rope and screamed at the ship. "Damn ye!" he shouted. "Damn ye, round up!"

I started down the leeward side. Crowe's boots were snared in the loops of rope, and he dragged great coils across the deck. "Ye devil!" he screamed at the schooner. "Ye soulless, black-hearted witch!"

"When you're through with that," I said, "I should like a word with you, *Captain* Crowe."

If he remembered those words from his first day on

the *Dragon,* he gave no sign of it. He whirled round, and even in that colorless light I could see the fire in his eyes.

"So that's it, is it?" he said. "I might have known ye'd come back. There's no getting rid of worms and rot."

Chapter 19
A HANGMAN'S NOOSE

I stopped only a few paces from Captain Crowe, the mast between us. "The *Dragon* is going to Dover," I said.

"Dover, is it?" He took a step back, a step sideways. I circled with him round the mast. "And who is it ye've got steering down there?"

"Fleming," I said.

Shocked, Crowe staggered back. He fell against the rail and caught himself with the preventer line.

"He came aboard in France. He was down below, in the place where you hid your smuggled spies."

"Damn ye," said Crowe.

"You heard him, didn't you? And you thought it was your son down there, tapping. Tapping for you."

"Och, ye're a half-wit," he said. "And Fleming too. Thirty years ago he was a half-wit, and he's no a day smarter."

"He's smart enough to take the *Dragon* from under your nose," I said. "He's smart enough to steer her."

"But do ye see where it is he's steering?"

"I told you," I said. "To Dover. To a hangman's noose for you."

"Look!" he shouted. "Does that look like Dover up there?"

I turned toward the bowsprit. There was nothing ahead but empty sea and a flock of gulls in the brightening sky. On the weather side — under the boom — the land was far away now, and passing at a furious rate.

"The Goodwin Sands are straight ahead," said Captain Crowe. "And he'll have us on them in an hour, at the rate the tide is making."

"You're lying," I said. "They're miles away."

"Ye can see the breakers now."

I was hardly aware of his movement. I stared at the sea, at row after row of waves growing smaller and darker as they stretched away, like a staircase laid from the sun. And with barely a twitch of his hand, Crowe freed the preventer, and the mainsail boom crashed across the deck.

I twisted away, but it struck my shoulder and sent me flying to the rail. I fell against the rack of belaying pins and slumped to the deck. Pain like none I'd ever felt coursed through my back and my arm.

"I'll kill ye," said Crowe. "I'll crush ye like a beetle, like a bumclock. Did ye think ye could get the better o' me? I've seen hundreds die, but none wi' the pleasure I'll feel in snapping your neck."

He came toward me, through the tangle of halyards. I

pulled myself up, and my hand found the belaying pin that held the mainsail's second halyard.

"I warned ye," he said. "Right from the start. 'Steer clear o' the *Dragon*,' I telt ye. See me hang? Ye won't live so long as that."

The *Dragon* lurched to leeward. It pressed me back against the rail, with a sudden tilting of the deck that might have been Fleming wrestling with the tiller or might have been the ship herself. Crowe lost his balance and fell into the heap of rope. And I snatched the pin from the rack.

The mainsail hurtled down the mast. Its enormous weight of canvas and wood, fully a ton or more, hauled both the halyards from the deck at a terrifying speed. They smoked through the blocks as the boom and the gaff and the canvas came tumbling down.

Crowe looked up. His face was a picture of fear. The line twisted round him, tangled and snarled. Loops opened and closed; they coiled round his neck. And all that weight of sail and wood drew the noose tight around him and yanked him from the deck.

Ten yards he rose in a second, kicking with his feet, clawing at the rope around his throat. And he hung there, turning slowly round to face the dawn. I thought back to Dasher's tale: *"It was a fine little jig he danced that night."*

I trembled with shock and relief. I let myself drop to the deck and looked at the sea, at the ship, at anything but the wretched corpse of Captain Crowe swinging high above me. I lay there, my back against the rail, and watched the colors come with the dawning of the day. And up from below came Fleming.

The *Dragon* slowly rounded up without him at the tiller. She sat with her topsail aback, jib and mainsail flapping. But I felt in no hurry to get her sailing again. I was happy enough to let her drift for a while.

"I told you so," said Fleming. "There you are, you see. Right to the dock. Right to—" He stopped. "Tell me this! Where the devil are we?"

"You steered the wrong way," I said.

He looked at me, at the snarls of rope, up at Captain Crowe. "He's dead. You killed him."

"I had to," I said.

"I didn't think it was possible." He went to the halyard and shook it. A curve of line, a wave, soared up and tapped at the captain's boots. Again he shook it, and again, and Crowe swung in his noose like a tolling bell. "You bastard," said Fleming. He screamed at the body, lashing with the line. "You wicked, wicked bastard! You took me life from me. You robbed me of all me years!"

I got up and led him away. He held on to me, sobbing, as I took him to the rail. "Look," I said. "The sun's rising now."

It came up from the sea, big and bright and gold. Fleming sniffed. He wiped his hand across the hairs that grew from his nose.

"Oh, it's beautiful," he said. "There's nothing like a sunrise. There's nothing so fine as a dawn."

"Are we near the Sands?" I asked. "The Goodwin Sands?"

Fleming squinted into the wind. His face was the same chalky white as the cliffs that lay to weather. "That's the

South Foreland there," he said, pointing. "Near the Sands? We've crossed them, boy. Aye, we've come right over the shoals."

It was true. In an arc across the stern, a mile or less behind us, the sea was brown and choppy. The tide rippled and leapt over banks of hidden sand.

"We should have been wrecked," I said. My hands were shaking. "It was sheer blind luck that saved us."

"Luck be damned." Fleming smiled. "It was the *Dragon*, boy. That devil, Crowe, had a hold of her heart. But she's free now, the poor old girl." He patted the top of her cabin. "Oh, she's a good old ship, and she'll take you far and look after you well."

We held no ceremony for Captain Crowe. We lowered his body, worked it loose, and heaved it over the side. There were no weights to take him down, no shroud to wrap him in. "I want to think that things are eating at him," Fleming said. "The birds and the fish and the worms." Then we connected the steering lines, hoisted the sails, and set a course for the Downs. The helm was loose and sloppy, but the *Dragon* didn't mind. She went home to the River Stour, to the same jetty that we'd started from. We had no anchor; we had to touch land.

And there to meet us was the boatman, the one-armed man who had taken my father and me out to the *Dragon* for the first time. He threw a springline round a bollard and brought the schooner to a stop. Then he stood and stared at me.

"Hallo!" I shouted.

"Oh, yes, I remember you." He spat in the water at the

Dragon's side. "Where's Turner Crowe? Where's Dasher and the others?"

"They're mostly dead," I told him. "Crowe and Mathew, and Harry too. I don't know what's become of Dasher."

He looked over the *Dragon* from bow to stern, from the severed cable to the broken foresail gaff, to the mainsail holed by a cannon shot. He pointed at me with his only arm. "Now don't try telling your father it was all like this before you left."

Chapter 20
ONE MORE NAME

I rode with Fleming, in a coach that took us south. All the way he gazed from the open window, marveling at everything.

"Smell the grass," he said. "Smell the trees." He took a great long breath, then blew it out. "Tell me this! Do we go through Canterbury?"

"No," I said. "It's the other way." It lay on the London road, the way I would have liked to go. But Fleming was dead set on taking me back to the Baskerville. "You can send for your father," he'd said. "You can wait for him there, and the two of you go on to London." It had seemed to me he was scared to go alone to a place—and a wife—he hadn't seen since before I was born.

We came up the bends of the river and on to Sandwich, in through the ancient wall. We passed the Weavers and the huge medieval churches, then hurried out through the wall again at a pace that was far too fast for Fleming.

"I imagine it's changed a lot," I said.

"Not at all," said he. "Not at all, now that I see it." He wore a grin as broad as his face. "Every night in me little prison bed I took this trip. North one night and south the next. I got meself in terrible muddles. Once I set off for Faversham, and you know how far that is."

Well, it was only a dozen miles. The coach could have carried us there in a little more than an hour.

"Long way to Faversham," said Fleming. He turned himself back to the window. "I lost meself out on the marsh."

We went through Deal and Walmer, and through the village of St. Margaret's. "I was married here," said Fleming, pointing to a towering steeple.

And then we were almost there. Fleming slouched in his seat, and for the first time in the journey we rode for a hundred yards without his talking at all.

"Are you worried?" I asked.

He nodded. "I'm older now," he said. "I don't want to see the look on her face when she gets an eyeful of all me wrinkles."

"She won't," I said. "She can't." It broke my heart to tell him she was blind.

"Blind?" He blinked at me. "You mean she can't see a thing?"

"I'm sorry," I said.

"No," said he. "It's fine. It's a blessing, maybe. That's what I think."

It was late in the evening when the coach pulled up at the Baskerville. We watched it go off down the road; then

Fleming took a moment to tidy himself. He tugged at his clothes; he smoothed down the hair at his ears and his nostrils. But still he stood at the inn door, staring at the latch. Then it clicked from within, and the door creaked open. And there was Mrs. Pye.

"Fleming?" she asked. "Is it you?"

"Aye, it's me." It was all he said. She flung herself at him, and he tried to hold her away to look at her, but she was seeing him with her hands. They went over his head and his face, over his shoulders and down his arms and up again. They were trembling, until he held them. For a moment the Pyes swayed together, shoulder to shoulder, hip to hip. They fitted like parts of a puzzle, the two of them withered and shrunken in the very same way. Then Fleming turned his head and smiled at me.

"You were right," said he. "She's as pretty as she ever was."

Father came the next day. We sat at the table where Captain Crowe had scattered out the Goodwin Sands with his bread crumbs. I told him all about the voyage. I admitted to the loss of an anchor.

"An anchor!" he said. "The devil with that. You could have lost the whole damn ship for all I care, so long as you came home yourself."

We made new plans in this place of our old ones. Mrs. Pye sat by the fire as Fleming brought us our glasses and supper.

"Do you want to say an end to this?" asked Father. "I

wouldn't blame you at all, young John. What is it they say: swallow the anchor? Come home to the business, and I'll hire a crew to take the *Dragon* over to the Indies."

"The Indies?" I said.

He nodded. "I found better buyers there for the wool. Twice the price they'd pay in London."

"But that's full across the ocean."

"A month away," said Father. "Another month back. It's what I mean, John. If you've had your fill of sailing, just say the word. There's a desk for you in London."

I said, "I'll need a new mainsail."

Father laughed. But in truth, it wasn't very jolly. "I suspected that was what you'd say." He pushed his chair back from the table. "All right, you can go. But this time, *you* hire the captain."

"That sits well with me," said I.

"Good." He slapped his hands on his knees. "Now let's have a look at this list of names."

I fetched the packet for him, and we went together through the book. It was even more stained than before, and we could barely make out half the names. But Crowe's was there, and Mathew's too. Harry's I wasn't sure about. And Dasher's? I searched for it from front to back, from back to front again. If Larson had written it there, not so much as a letter was left to be read.

"Well," said Father. "That's one who'll escape the noose."

I told him what Dasher had asked me: *"If you see I'm not there, will you write me in? Will you do that, John?"* Father was happy to oblige. He sent Fleming for a quill, and he added to the list of smugglers' names that of Dashing Tommy Dusker. Then he licked his fingers and smudged the ink; he blotted the book on his napkin.

"There," he said. "I've never been happier to do a turn for a scoundrel."

We left the Baskerville that same night, and the sounds of the sea soon fell away behind us. We would go together as far as Canterbury; then Father would stay on for London and a trip to the Old Bailey. I would go east, back to the *Dragon*.

"I'm proud of you," said Father as we rolled along. "Proud as Punch."

The carriage banged and jostled down a hill, around a corner into the forest. I swayed in the seat and pressed against my father. I didn't have to; we weren't going all that fast. But I felt too old to hug him simply from affection.

The coach shimmied and steadied. Then above the pounding of the horses' hooves came a pistol shot. Another. And a voice I knew all too well shouted out, "Stand and deliver!"

"Oh, Lord," said Father. "Not again."

"It's all right." I leaned over him and poked my head out the window. "Carry on, driver," I said. "Don't bother stopping."

He cracked his whip, and the horses broke to a gallop. The wind rushed past me, smelling of leaves and grass. I saw Dasher ahead, in a pool of moonlight.

"Hold up there!" he cried. "Hold up there, I tell you!"

Then we whistled past him, and he saw me at the window. "Lord love me, it's John!" he said, and his voice followed us through the forest.

"Tell them in London that Dashing Tommy Dusker let you go safe! You hear me? Tell them he spared you!" His words were growing faint. "Good luck to you, John. May the fates make us shipmates again."

AUTHOR'S NOTE

Wherever there are borders, there are smugglers to cross them, making money by avoiding the taxes and the duties paid by honest people. Smuggling is an old profession, even older than the word itself. Three hundred years ago, the men who carried tobacco, tea, and silk across the English Channel were known as smuckelers. They smuckeled their cargos into England with little danger of arrest or punishment.

In those days the "free trade" was done very much in the open, and many coastal villages owned and outfitted small fleets of boats that shuttled back and forth across the Channel. So great was the gain, and so small the danger, that smuggling grew to a gigantic industry.

Around the beginning of the eighteenth century, the government of England took steps to stop the smugglers. Preventive forces were established, first on land and then at sea. Penalties became harsher. And smuggling changed to a deadly business.

At the time this story is set, the start of the nineteenth century, a smuggling run would draw farmhands from their fields, blacksmiths from their forges, and bakers from their ovens. They would show up for a night of work and go back to their jobs in the daylight. At dawn the farmer might find his horse with muddied hooves, but there would be a keg of brandy left beside the stable door. And he would take his payment and look the other way; the smuggling gangs were known for their violence, and it was better not to cross them.

The English poet Rudyard Kipling wrote about that in his haunting "A Smuggler's Song," in which a parent warns a child not to listen to the noises of the night and tells her to "watch the wall, my darling, while the Gentlemen go by!"

But smuggling was going through a change at this time. The large masses of men who did their work by force were being replaced by smaller groups who used trickery instead. Some of their schemes sound more like fiction than fact: hollow masts stuffed with tea; tobacco woven to look like ropes, then laid among the real cables in the ship's dark locker; weighted barrels that could be sunk offshore and harvested later by little fishing smacks; floating barrels painted to look like innocent buoys. As Dasher describes it for John, the smugglers sometimes buried their cargos under reeking loads of rotten fish, or fitted out their boats with elaborate and secret compartments. The smuggler *Good Intent* had a pipe that ran from her deck right through her hull, so that a raft of barrels could be tied to a rope and hauled tight against her bottom. Silk was stuffed inside the skins of hams. The smugglers themselves might carry packets of tea under their capes or inside their petticoat trousers.

Most of these devices came along well after the time of Dasher and Captain Crowe. But they are part of the history now, part of the folklore, and I believe I might be forgiven for smuggling them into the story.

It is true that smugglers carried spies in the war between England and France. Napoleon himself admitted it: "Most of the information I received from England came through the smugglers. They are people who have courage and the ability to do anything for money."

And that is something that's still true today, when smugglers are more likely to carry drugs than tea. Small boats sailing down the coasts of Central and South America are sometimes warned to stay well offshore and to keep their boats darkened in the night. And if a boat goes by at enormous speed or a voice hails you from the darkness, the wisest thing to do is still to turn and watch the wall as the gentlemen go by.

Books about smugglers can be found in nearly every library and bookstore. A good one to look for is *Smugglers' Britain,* by the English writer Richard Platt. And for fiction, try *Moonfleet,* an old story by John Meade Falkner that scared my father as a boy and then scared me, and is now scaring his grandchildren at my brother's home in Ontario, very far from the sea.

ACKNOWLEDGMENTS

Many of my favorite parts of *The Smugglers* spring from the efforts of other people. Captain Crowe's more colorful comments were spoken first by my mother, who gave me—in my infancy—a thick Highland brogue that I'm sometimes told has not completely disappeared. Dasher's most eloquent phrases, and most of the research material, came from my father, who was born in an English inn with a timbered parlor that I can only imagine was much like the Baskerville. Young John's father comes teetering out of my first novel and into this one on a walking stick thanks to the inspiration of Kristin Miller, who has shared my life for a dozen years. The head of the smuggling gang appears with his sword and his fancy clothes through the suggestions of Lauri Hornik, who edited this book as carefully and thoughtfully as she did *The Wreckers*. The stern chase across the Channel occurs through the research of librarian Kathleen Larkin, who finds answers for me to the most obscure of questions. And the whole story exists partly because of the encouragement of my agent, Jane Jordan Browne, to whom I owe an awful lot.

Thanks for *The Smugglers* also go to Bruce Wishart, who plundered his library to answer many questions; to Barry

White, who trekked around London looking for charts of the Goodwin Sands; and to Richard Hunn, who described for me the Kentish coast that he knew from his boyhood.

And, finally, I have to thank everyone who has told me that he or she has read and enjoyed *The Wreckers*, but most of all my nephews and my nieces. They turned a sailboat into a madhouse for a summer voyage in search of whales. And for the pleasure they brought me, and the inspiration to carry on, I have dedicated this book to them.

John Spencer's adventures conclude
in *The Buccaneers*.
Turn the page for a sample chapter
from that exciting companion novel.

0-440-41671-X

A Dell Yearling Book

Chapter 1
THE LIFEBOAT

I was steering the *Dragon* when the lifeboat came into view.

It appeared ahead, a tattered sail on a sea that blazed with the evening sun. Its canvas bleached to white, its hull bearded with weeds, it looked as ancient as Moses. But it drove into the teeth of the trade winds, beating toward a land so distant that there might have been no land at all.

I felt a shiver to see such a tiny craft in such an endless waste of sea and sky. We were twenty-one days out of England, a thousand miles from any shore. But even our schooner—a little world for the eight of us aboard—seemed almost too small for the ocean.

"Sail!" I shouted, and turned the wheel. "Sail ho!"

The *Dragon* leaned under her press of canvas. With a boom and a shudder she swallowed a wave in the huge carved mouth of her figurehead. Men stirred from the deck, rising to tend the sails, and the sounds of stomping feet and squealing rope brought Captain Butterfield up from below.

The sun glinted through his graying hair and onto the pink of his scalp as he stooped through the companionway. "What's the matter, John?" he asked.

"A boat, sir." I pointed forward.

He'd brought his spyglass, and he aimed it at the distant lifeboat.

"How many people?" I asked.

He took a moment to answer. "None," he said.

"That's impossible," I told him.

He lowered the glass, wiped his eye, and looked again. The long lens stayed perfectly still as his arms and his knees bent with the roll of the ship. Then he brought it down and shook his head. "Look for yourself."

He traded the glass for the wheel, and it was all I could do to keep that glass aimed at the lifeboat. But I had to agree: there seemed to be no one aboard.

"Can we fire a gun?" I asked.

"Good thinking, John." He shouted for the gunner. "Mr. Abbey! A signal, please."

For the first time in our voyage, I was glad we had our four little guns and the little man who worked them, as strange as he was. He stripped the crisp tarpaulin jacket from the nearest cannon, and had it ready to fire so quickly that I realized only then that he'd kept it loaded all the way from London.

A cloud of smoke barked from the gun. The *Dragon* shook from stem to stern, and the lifeboat flew from the circle of sea in my spyglass. Then I found it again, and there was a man staring at me, peering past the edge of the sail. He had been sitting to leeward, with that tattered rag of a sail as a shelter from the spray and sun.

"There, he's seen us," I shouted.

"And look!" cried Captain Butterfield. "Good heavens, he's turning away."

It was true. The man had put up the helm of his little boat and it now spun toward the south. As we watched, he eased the sheets and ducked his head as the sail billowed out above him. Then off he went, fleeing as fast as he could from the only bit of help that he had in all the world.

"Confound him," said Butterfield. "Is he mad?"

I thought he must have been. I saw his head looking back, turning on shoulders as broad as a bull's. Then, just as quickly, he put his helm over again, and came racing toward us.

"Heave to!" shouted Butterfield. "Best we let the devil come to us."

We turned the *Dragon* into the wind and lashed her wheel. She lay almost dead in the water, scudding sideways as the swells rolled underneath her. The captain and I—like every man aboard—stood by the rail and watched that lifeboat crawl up to weather.

Its paint long gone, its seams plugged by scraps of cloth, it looked like a feast for the sea worms. Tangles of weeds trailed in its wake; water slopped in its bilge. But the man who sailed it was bronzed and strong, as though he'd set out just the day before to sail across an ocean.

An enormous sea chest of polished wood was jammed between the thwarts.

He brought his boat alongside, cast off his sheet, and dropped the tiller. Then he hoisted that great box onto his shoulder and climbed up to the deck of the *Dragon*.

"Help him below," said Butterfield. "Give him a meal and a hammock."

"Aye, sir," I said.

The men scattered as I went forward, the hands to the sails, Abbey to his gun. Only the stranger was left, sitting astride his chest and looking very much at home. His hair was tarred in a pigtail, and though his skin was deeply tanned, his eyes were a very clear blue.

"Where have you come from?" I asked.

"From the sea," he said. And that was all. He came to his feet, towering above me, and glanced up at the topsail, aft to the stern—everywhere but down at his boat, which wallowed in the swells as we left it behind.

I bent to take the man's sea chest, the finest one I'd ever seen. The rope beckets—the handles—were so elaborately knotted that months of work must have passed in their making. The wood glowed with its warm finish of oil. But I grunted at the weight of it. Though stronger than most boys of seventeen, I couldn't hope to lift that enormous box.

The stranger laughed and put it up to his shoulder again. The sound that came from inside it—a rumbling and a clinking—made me think that coins and jewels were nested there. Then he followed me down to the fo'c's'le, where I hung a hammock that he climbed into without a word of thanks.

"Would you like some food?" I asked. "Some water?"

He shook his head, his eyes already closed. In another moment he was sound asleep, swinging in the canvas as though in the great cocoon of some enormous insect.

I found a blanket and covered him, then went up to help Mr. Abbey secure the gun. We stretched the tarpaulin jacket in place and lashed it down.

"There you go," said Abbey, stroking at the cloth, smoothing it over the muzzle. "You rest awhile." He had a habit of talking to his guns, and it always unnerved me. "That will keep you dry, my handsome little man-eater," he said.

He loved his guns, but I despised them. Their weight made the *Dragon* roll badly at times, and only batter through waves she would have hurdled without them. But my father had insisted on arming the *Dragon,* and whether or not to carry guns was the only decision he hadn't left to me. "You're going to the Indies," he'd said. "There's pirates in the Indies."

I laughed now, to think of that. What a dreadful place the West Indies had seemed from the way Father had described them. He'd filled the waters with sharks and wood-eating worms, the sky with hurricanes that blew all the year round, and the islands with swarms of cannibals. "Yes, cannibals," he'd said. "They cook you alive, or so I've heard. They shrink your head to the size of a walnut."

But his fear of pirates had been the greatest of all, and he'd paid a fortune for the little four-pounders that sat on the deck, two to a side, with their muzzles pointing over the rail. Then, true to form, he'd found a bargain in the gunner. "Same wages as an ordinary seaman," he'd boasted. "Yet the man was serving in the navy before you were born." So great was Father's love of bargains that he overlooked Mr. Abbey's years, his oddness, even the glass marble fitted in place of his left eye, in a head as round as a cannonball.

That marble gleamed crimson now, as Abbey looked up from the lashings. The sun was turning red, staining the sails. It lit a blaze right across the horizon, scattering embers of light on the sea.

"I don't like the looks of him," he said.

"Who?" I asked.

"That fellow from the lifeboat. Where did he come from and where was he bound?"

"I'm sure I don't know, Mr. Abbey," I said.

"Why was he sailing into the wind?" Abbey tilted his head. "I'd ask him that, if I were you, Mr. Spencer. I'd ask him why he was tacking east when he might have run to the west, where the land was closer."

"Perhaps you'll ask him yourself," I said. Then I turned away and stood at the rail.

"Count on it, Mr. Spencer."

I didn't care very much for the gunner. He still sported the rags of his old naval uniform, and seemed to think that his faded gold braid and his little brass buttons made him equal to an admiral.

"I'll ask him this as well," he said, coming up to my side. "I'll ask him what he carries in that bureau of his."

I laughed. The stranger's sea chest was enormous, but not quite as big as a bureau.

"I think he's a Jonah, maybe," said Abbey.

"That's absurd," I said.

"Is it? Does he look like a man who's been adrift for weeks?"

"Perhaps he hasn't been," I said.

Abbey grunted. "But his boat has."

I wouldn't admit it to Abbey, but I'd had the same thought. The boat had grown weak, but the man was still strong.

"Try it," said Abbey. "Get into a boat and drift out there. In a matter of days, the sun turns you into a cinder. In a fortnight it makes a mummy of you, dry as old leather." He spat into the sea. "A man outlive his boat? Not a chance!"

His one good eye was closed, yet he stared straight at me with the reflected sunset glaring in his glass marble. It was a most disturbing thing, as though he could actually see with some kind of fiery vision.

"Look in his sea chest," said Abbey. "If he's a Jonah, he'll carry his curses in there."

"That's enough!" I said.

Abbey cackled. He turned his head and looked down at the sea. The water seethed below us, and the *Dragon* churned on toward the west. She rushed down a wave, rose on the face of the next. The sun flared once more and disappeared. And Mr. Abbey gasped.

He reached out and clutched my arm. "Did you see that?" he cried.

"What?" I asked.

"Right there!" he shouted. "You must have seen it." He stretched over the rail, staring straight down at the sea, then aft along the hull. He squeezed shivers of pain into my arm. "Tell me you did."

"See what?" I asked again.

"A coffin," he cried. "It looked like a coffin all nailed together, the lid swinging open." He stared at me with utter horror. "Tell me you saw it."

I tried to shake him off, but his fingers held me like talons. "I saw no such thing," I said.

"Then I'm doomed!" He let me go and slumped at the rail. "I'm finished. We all are, maybe."

"No one's doomed," said I.

His glass eye burned. "Oh, we are, young Mr. Spencer. There's a Jonah come aboard."

ABOUT THE AUTHOR

Iain Lawrence was born in Ontario, Canada. A former journalist, he now writes full-time. In addition to his magazine and newspaper articles, he is the author of two nonfiction books about sailing and the novel *The Wreckers*, which was a *School Library Journal* Best Book of the Year, a *Bulletin* Blue Ribbon book, and a *Booklist* Editors' Choice book, and for which he was named a *Publishers Weekly* Flying Start author.

An avid sailor who enjoys building ships in bottles, Iain Lawrence spends several months every year traveling by boat with his longtime companion, Kristin, and their dog, the Skipper. Their home is a remote radio-transmission site on an island off Prince Rupert, on the north coast of British Columbia.

DATE DUE
